He planted his hand on the picnic blanket behind her and she rested back against his shoulder, a comfortable position reminiscent of previous picnics.

She sipped the remains of her apple juice. "I'd forgotten how much I love it here."

"Me, too." His head almost touched hers and he turned toward her, his breath warm on her ear. "Have I told you how beautiful you are?"

She sucked in a deep breath, her pulse rate accelerating. His words awakened responses she hadn't experienced since she'd left him years ago. "Not today."

His fingers caressed her cheek, tucking a few loose strands of hair behind her ears. "You always look stunning."

"Hardly." She giggled. "My hair is a disaster, and frizzy after the swim."

He shook his head, his fingers entwined in her hair at the nape of her neck. "Your hair is lovely."

She leaned toward him, her eyes locked in his intense gaze. "I've missed this. You and me together, like old times."

"Yes." His eyes darkened, and the hand entangled in her hair drew her head closer. "We shared some memorable moments."

Books by Narelle Atkins

Love Inspired Heartsong Presents

Falling for the Farmer
The Nurse's Perfect Match
The Doctor's Return

NARELLE ATKINS

lives in Canberra, Australia, with her husband and children. Her love of romance novels was inspired by her grandmother's extensive collection. After discovering inspirational romances, she decided to write stories of faith and romance. A regular at her local gym, she also enjoys traveling and spending time with family and friends.

NARELLE ATKINS

The Doctor's Return

HEARTSONG
PRESENTS

Recycling programs
for this product may
not exist in your area.

™ LOVE INSPIRED BOOKS

ISBN-13: 978-0-373-48722-6

THE DOCTOR'S RETURN

Copyright © 2014 by Narelle Atkins

www.Harlequin.com

Printed in U.S.A.

There is a time for everything, and a season for every activity under the heavens.
—*Ecclesiastes* 3:1

For my writing sister Dorothy Adamek,
who provided unending support during the writing
of this book. And my dear reader friend and
Australian Christian Readers Blog Alliance cofounder
Jenny Blake, who helped name characters in this story
and brainstorm a couple of scenes.

A big thank-you to my wonderful critique partners
Susan Diane Johnson and Stacy Monson. Your input
is invaluable. I thank my reader friends for their
helpful comments and support: Jen B, Lisa B,
Raylee B, Karinne C, Tracey H, Daniela M,
Heather M, Merlyn S and Nicky S.

Chapter 1

Megan Bradley inhaled the sweet perfume of a champagne rose in her sister-in-law's garden. "Kate, I love your roses. Jack has outdone himself this time."

Kate smiled. "A belated wedding present but definitely worth the wait."

Megan's brother had planted the rose garden along one side of the newly built home on the family apple farm in Snowgum Creek. After a number of delays, the house had been completed a couple of months ago, but Kate's debilitating morning sickness had postponed their Saturday lunch housewarming until today.

Megan stretched out the muscles in her back, stiff after yesterday's long drive from Sydney. Family and friends gathered on the spacious wooden deck at the back of the sandy brick house overlooking the Snowy Mountains. Only one person was missing—her brother's best friend, Luke Morton. She needed to summon the courage to talk to Luke soon.

She lifted her arms above her head, releasing tension in her shoulders. "As much as I'd love to hide away and chat, we should mingle with your guests."

Kate nodded. "I've been ordered to take it easy. Your mom and Aunt Doris have taken over my kitchen, and Jack is in charge of our new outdoor grill."

Megan straightened the hem of her lilac shirt. "They won't stop fussing over you until the baby arrives." She grinned. "I can't wait to meet my little nephew or niece."

Kate placed her hand on her slightly rounded abdomen. "Hopefully bub won't arrive early. I'd like some time to get settled in the house first."

A black Jeep meandered along a narrow dirt track leading to the house. Megan sucked in a deep breath, her pulse skyrocketing.

Kate lifted a brow. "I told you Luke was coming."

"I know." A busy doctor, Luke Morton had probably been delayed at the Snowgum Creek Medical Clinic. "I need to ask Jack something." She strode toward the back deck, away from Luke, who had parked his Jeep under a gum tree near the front of the house.

Kate followed close on her heels. "You can't run away from him forever."

"I'm not running." She frowned. Who was she kidding? She'd spent eight years trying to forget the events that had transpired the last time she'd seen him. "And I will talk to him today." Assuming he was willing to talk to her.

Megan left Kate chatting with friends and walked over to her brother. Jack stood near the grill on the far side of the deck, a broad smile covering his tanned face. She was glad he'd married her best friend a few years ago, and that he now looked forward to becoming a father later this year.

She breathed in the tantalizing aroma of barbecued beef. "Something smells good." Rib-eye steaks sizzled on the grill.

Jack nodded. "Lunch is nearly ready." He turned over a couple of steaks. "How are you?"

She pasted a bright smile on her face. "I'm fine. A bit tired from the drive yesterday." She'd arrived after dinner, exhausted from her last-minute rush yesterday morning to pack up all her belongings in her Chatswood apartment.

"How long are you visiting with Mom and Dad?"

"I'm not sure." Her family was unaware of her potential job opportunities and the strong possibility she might live in Snowgum Creek for the next twelve months. The longest period she would live in one place since she'd completed her exercise physiology studies in Sydney eight years before.

His lips formed a wry smile. "Luke is heading our way."

Megan spun around and flicked her long dark hair back over her shoulders. Luke's golden-brown eyes met her gaze, his face devoid of emotion as he wove his way through the guests gathering around tables on the deck.

She wiped clammy hands down the sides of her designer-label black fitted pants, holding his gaze and refusing to look away first. Her heart danced to a faster beat as old feelings, long forgotten, washed over her. He was leaner and fitter than she remembered, decked out in a casual shirt and jeans. His face had matured and his honey-brown hair was cropped short. No surprise he was considered the most eligible bachelor in Snowgum Creek.

Jack stepped forward and shook Luke's hand, stealing his attention. "Glad you could make it."

"Sorry I'm late. I had to fit in a couple of extra patients."

"No worries, we're just about to sit down and eat."

Luke turned to Megan, his intense gaze searching her face. "It's been a long time."

"Yep." She nibbled her lower lip, words escaping her. He still had the ability to scatter her thoughts.

Jack cleared his throat. "I'll be back in a few minutes."

Luke nodded. "Do you need me to do anything?"

"Can you watch the grill? We're putting the meat platters on the tables."

"No problem." Luke picked up an empty white ceramic platter.

"Thanks." Jack stepped away from the grill. "I think we're organized and ready to serve lunch."

Her brother headed indoors and an awkward silence followed Jack's departure. Luke filled a couple of platters with juicy steaks and she distributed the platters to nearby tables.

She lingered beside the grill. "Is there anything else I can do?"

"No, I think we're all right." He added a row of steaks to the grill. "You're looking well." Luke's eyes softened, his velvet voice sending her pulse into overdrive.

"Thanks." She twisted a lock of hair around her finger. "I hear you've taken over Dr. Davidson's medical clinic."

"He retired last year, and the clinic provided a great opportunity to move back home from Sunny Ridge."

"That makes sense." His dream eight years ago had been to finish med school and own a medical clinic in Snowgum Creek. A dream she hadn't shared. Her yearning had been to travel and explore the world.

"I'm glad to be back. Snowgum Creek is a thriving town, unlike many small towns in this region."

"Kate said Sunny Ridge is booming, too."

"It has experienced significant growth over the last decade." He checked the remaining steaks on the grill. "Did you know Sunny Ridge is now officially classified as a city?"

"Really?" She inspected her fingernails. They'd need a manicure if she helped Jack and his workers pick the last of the apple crop next week. "I heard your medical clinic is expanding."

"Yes. It keeps me busy. My schedule this morning was jam-packed and I ran overtime."

"Is that normal?"

"Sometimes. It depends on the day."

Jack returned and Luke handed over the cooking utensils.

"Thanks." Jack smiled. "You two should sit down and enjoy lunch."

Luke turned toward her, indicating two spare seats at a nearby table. "Would you like to join me?"

"Sure." He held out a chair and she slipped into the wooden seat. How many times had they practiced this ritual during their four-year relationship in college?

Luke sat beside her and together they served their lunch of steak, salad and crusty French bread rolls. Megan made small talk with a couple of Jack's friends who she hadn't seen in years. Her short visits back home over the past eleven years hadn't included catching up with the townsfolk. Luke seemed at ease beside her, chatting with the other guests.

His forearm brushed against her elbow and she tensed, aware of his presence only inches away. She concentrated on her lunch, her traitorous heart liking his close proximity. The moment everyone at their table had finished, she stood and started clearing their plates.

"I'll help." Luke collected a few empty platters and walked with her to the kitchen.

Alone with Luke, she focused on loading the plates and cutlery into the dishwasher.

He leaned back against the kitchen counter, arms crossed over his muscular chest. "Are you here for the weekend or longer?"

"I haven't decided."

"Did you take leave from work?"

She shook her head. "I'm between jobs at the moment.

Please pass on my congratulations to Ben and Amy, by the way."

"I will. They arrived back from their honeymoon a few weeks ago."

"Where did they go?"

"Batemans Bay, one of Ben's favorite fishing spots. They were supposed to be here today but my niece is sick with a cold."

"I hope she gets well soon." She pulled out the top rack, already half-full with cups and glasses. "Um, can we talk?"

"Sure, what about?"

"No, not here. Can we go somewhere where we won't be overheard?"

He raised an eyebrow. "It has taken you long enough to finally decide to talk."

Touché. She lowered her lashes, knowing she had hurt him. At least he was prepared to talk.

"How about a walk in the orchards?" he asked.

Like old times. How often had they snuck away into the orchards? Her cheeks flushed as memories of her final year of high school invaded her thoughts.

She squared her shoulders. "I'll finish cleaning the kitchen first."

"I'll meet you at my Jeep in ten minutes." A smile curved up the corners of his lips. "If we're not discreet, the gossips will have us married off by the end of the afternoon."

"True, they don't need any encouragement."

"See you soon." He left the kitchen, his boots tapping on the wooden floorboards as he headed toward the veranda.

She filled the top rack with cups and bowls from the sink and switched on the dishwasher. Luke seemed okay with her temporary return to Snowgum Creek, but was he prepared to make this a more permanent arrangement? Could she convince him to rent her a consulting room in his medical clinic?

Ten minutes later, Luke let himself out the front door of Jack and Kate's home and headed over to his Jeep. He walked around the vehicle and found Megan slouched against the door, her beautiful dark blue eyes squinting in the early-afternoon sunlight.

His heart constricted, bittersweet memories filling his mind. Jack had warned him that she'd be here today, but he hadn't been prepared for the deluge of feelings that had smashed through him when his gaze had locked with hers. Eight years had passed, and he still wasn't immune to her charms.

"Which way should we walk?" he asked.

She stood straighter, rolling her shoulders. "Toward the pine trees."

He nodded. The obvious solution since that part of the orchard wasn't visible from the house. He fell into step with her, his curiosity building. Why had she sought him out after all these years?

They walked between rows of apple trees, passing wombat burrows on the edge of the path.

He ducked under a low-lying apple branch, heavy with ripe fruit. "Do emus still visit the dam?"

She shrugged. "You'll have to ask Jack."

He remembered hiding with her at the far end of the orchard and watching a pair of emus skirt around the dam, their heads bobbing on their long necks as they walked. Occasionally a platypus would pop its head out of the water. Kangaroos had bounded through the orchards at dawn and dusk. Scare guns had echoed at regular intervals, deterring the cockatoos and other birds from feasting on the apples.

The breeze lifted her glossy hair off her shoulders, a few wisps blowing in front of her face. She looked exactly the same as he'd remembered, with only a couple of fine lines now crinkling at the corners of her eyes when she smiled. Her face was lightly tanned and her body toned, presumably from regular workout sessions at the gym.

"What do you want to talk about?" he asked.

She pressed her lips together. "My work."

Kate had told him about Megan's nomadic lifestyle. Ski instructor at the Snowy Mountains every winter, and short-term exercise physiology contract work in Sydney fitted in around overseas trips. "You must be heading off to the snow soon."

"Actually, I'm not going this year."

He paused, turning to face her. "But you go to the snow every year."

She stared at the ground, kicking a stick with her black leather boot.

He frowned. Something didn't add up. She had been obsessed with skiing for as long as he could remember. He had it on good authority from Kate that she loved her regular ski instructor job at the Snowy Mountains resort village.

"Are you injured?"

Her eyes widened. "Physically I'm fine and my knees are in good shape." She traced her finger over a ripe Granny Smith apple hanging on a low branch. "It's time for a change, that's all."

She wasn't telling him the full story but it wasn't his prerogative to push for information. Eight years ago she had made his place in her life crystal clear.

She drew in a deep breath. "I'm looking to stay in Snow-gum Creek for a while."

He narrowed his eyes. "What does that have to do with me?"

"I've been offered a contract with Sunny Ridge and Snowgum Creek hospitals."

"I'm glad to hear they're planning to expand their services." Many of his elderly patients struggled to travel for two hours to Sunny Ridge to access essential health services that weren't available in Snowgum Creek.

She nodded. "They're very keen to employ me but only for three days a week. One day a week in Sunny Ridge, where the job is based, and two days in Snowgum Creek. I would need a second job to supplement my income."

"Have you heard the health club has been redeveloped?"

"Yes. Kate is very excited about the new facilities."

"The townsfolk spent a couple of years lobbying and fund-raising to build the facility. The hospital has access to the heated pool." It seemed as though everyone in town had a stake in the new fitness center and indoor pool complex.

"Another reason why they are prepared to employ an exercise physiologist who works at both hospitals."

"That makes sense. From what I've seen, the gym facilities would suit rehab patients."

She nodded. "I'm looking to set up my own business, consulting to private patients and personal training at the gym. I need to rent a consulting room a few days a week, and you own the only medical clinic in town with extra space."

His mouth fell open. She wanted to work with him in his clinic. He stood taller, shaking his head. "I do want to lease the space but I'm looking for long-term tenants."

"I'm prepared to sign a twelve-month contract with an option to extend."

"Seriously?" She was prepared to live in one place for a whole year? He had his doubts.

"The hospital contract is for a year minimum."

"What about skiing? And overseas holidays?" Could she sacrifice her jet-setting lifestyle and settle in a small town?

"It can wait." She placed her hands on her hips and lifted her chin. "I'm committed to this new direction for my life."

He tugged his mouth into a firm line. "You know you can't leave your patients and clients without care if you decide to run off overseas or to the ski slopes for a few months. And since I'm going to be one of the doctors referring patients to you, I need to feel confident you'll be around to look after them."

Her wide eyes pleaded for his understanding. "All I can give you is my word. I know why you think I'm unreliable...."

He rubbed his hand through his hair. "This is a business decision." A decision clouded by his personal judgments and past experiences.

"There are currently no exercise physiologists in Snowgum Creek." She sighed. "You know the health club is fully equipped to suit my needs. I promise you, I'm not going to run off in breach of my contracts."

Unlike the way she ran off the night he'd proposed marriage. A week later she was in Whistler, Canada, at a ski resort. He'd been a struggling med student who would have done anything for her, made enormous sacrifices to keep her happy. Instead, he'd learned the hard way that she was more committed to her freedom than to him.

Now their lives had intersected on an unfamiliar path, and she was the one asking him for favors. Despite being drawn to her, he couldn't risk his heart by getting involved again. Working with her, seeing her on a regular basis, would be an added complication.

He couldn't ignore the fact that his patients were on

waiting lists for services Megan could provide. Services they might not receive if he declined Megan's request and she chose to leave Snowgum Creek. "Okay, I'll think about it." *Against my better judgment.*

She smiled, her face vibrant in the afternoon sunlight. "Thank you. I appreciate your help and I won't let you down."

"It's not a done deal yet, and I need to talk to my legal people first." He tipped his head to the side. "Do you really want a one-year contract with an option to negotiate an extension?"

"Yes, please." Her blue eyes gleamed. "I promise you won't regret this."

He swallowed hard. Could he put aside their past history and build a successful working relationship for the benefit of the Snowgum Creek community? Could he afford not to?

Chapter 2

Megan climbed a ladder and picked succulent green apples from the high branches in the family orchard. Her neck and back muscles strained from the pressure of holding the apples in a padded canvas fruit-picking bucket. The cumbersome bucket rested against her flat stomach, held in place by a harness strapped over her shoulders.

After three days in the orchard, she now remembered how physically taxing it was to pick apples. She climbed down, detached the bottom of the bucket and deposited the apples in a nearby wooden crate.

Jack rode by on his four-wheel motorbike, a full bin of apples attached to a trailer. He cut the engine and jumped off the bike. "How's it going?"

She adjusted her baseball cap and wiped the back of her hand over her sweaty forehead. "I'm getting a good workout."

He peered into her apple bin. "You're doing well. I'd forgotten how fast you are at picking."

"I'm sure you're much quicker than me these days. I'm out of practice." She hadn't picked apples since her university days when she'd come home for the long weekend Easter break.

"But you're still a good worker."

She wiped dust off her sunglass lenses using the hem

of her T-shirt. "I'm earning my keep until I start the hospital job."

"So you signed the hospital contract?"

"I sure did, and Luke is drawing up a contract for the medical clinic." She was thankful Luke had agreed to let her work with him at the clinic.

"It will be good to have you around when the baby arrives."

"Yep." She grabbed her water bottle and drank a few mouthfuls, the cool liquid satisfying her thirst.

"I'd better keep moving and check up on my other pickers to see if they're working as hard as you."

"Not a chance." She returned to the tree, spotting a couple of apples she'd missed. If only the Granny Smith apples didn't blend in with the leaves.

She worked her way along her row of trees, enjoying the fresh mountain air and the sunlight on her face. Later that week she planned to purchase a health club membership and resume her rigorous indoor fitness regimen. She couldn't expect to recruit personal training clients if she didn't train regularly and look the part.

She climbed down the ladder, balancing her load of apples.

A familiar deep voice halted her progress to the apple bin. "Hey, Megan, is Jack cracking the whip and putting you to work?"

Luke ducked under a branch and joined her, a wide grin on his face. He wore a business shirt and long pants, sunglasses shading his eyes.

She smiled and pulled her baseball cap lower over her face. "I'm having fun." No doubt she looked a mess, wearing an old T-shirt and shorts streaked with dirt. Her mother had insisted she apply a generous layer of pink zinc cream to protect her face from the sun. "You could always roll up your sleeves and give me a hand."

He laughed. "Ben has already tried that one on me today, with no success. I've left your lease agreement with your mother."

"Thanks." She waddled over to the crate and released her load of apples into the bin. "I'll look at it tonight and get back to you."

"No worries." He paused. "I was wondering if you've decided where you're going to live."

She shook her head, moving on to the next tree. "I'll stay with Mom and Dad until I find a rental."

"Ben mentioned that Amy is looking to rent out her cottage soon, and she's planning to lease it partly furnished."

"It sounds like a possibility." She'd been staying with her parents for less than a week and she was already keen to have her own space as soon as possible. She loved her parents and knew they had her best interests at heart, but her mom's fussing and inquisitive questions tested her patience.

"I'll let Amy know you may be interested." He shoved his hands in his pockets, rocking back and forward on his heels. "By the way, I missed seeing you at church on Sunday."

Her grip tightened on an apple, and she wrenched the stalk harder than necessary. "I slept in."

"Maybe I'll see you next Sunday."

She shrugged. "I don't often make it to church."

"Really? When we were at university you seemed very committed."

"Times change, I guess." She reached for another apple on a low branch. "I move around a lot and haven't found the right church." She also hadn't felt the need to attend church services on a regular basis. A fact her mother had reminded her of too many times this past week. She sensed her aunt Doris didn't approve of her nomadic lifestyle, but at least she'd kept her opinions to herself and hadn't pressured her to comply with her standards.

He frowned, checking his watch. "Yes, a lot has changed. I need to get back to the clinic."

"Okay. Thanks again for bringing over the contract."

"No problem. I'll see you later." He waved goodbye and strode away toward the house.

She repositioned the ladder, ready to climb to the top. Kate had told her all about the lovely and welcoming people who belonged to Snowgum Creek Community Church. It wouldn't hurt to start attending services again at her old church. It would pacify her mother and provide another opportunity to see Luke.

Despite their complicated history, she couldn't help feeling drawn to him. Curiosity drove her to learn more about his life in Snowgum Creek. Why did he seem content to settle in their hometown when his medical background provided numerous opportunities to travel and work in more exotic locations?

Luke walked between rows of apple trees, his brows drawn together. Megan's attitude toward church had surprised him. She'd been enthusiastic about her faith in her youth, and he'd never have predicted her faith would become lukewarm in her twenties. Her evasive answers affirmed his belief that she was a fun-loving girl who enjoyed her freedom and avoided responsibilities.

He reached his Jeep and spotted Jack heading his way.

Jack waved and pulled his four-wheel motorbike to a stop beside the Jeep. "Do you have time for coffee?"

"Not today." He pulled his car keys out of his pocket,

beeping the vehicle open. "I'm due back at the clinic, and I only stopped by to drop off Megan's contract."

"So, you're really going to do it?"

"Yep. It's a done deal after she signs on the dotted line."

Jack let the motorbike engine idle, and tipped his head to the side. "My sister is full of surprises."

He swung open the door of his Jeep. "She says she's determined to stay for at least a year."

"To be honest, I'm puzzled by her change of heart." Jack rubbed his hand along his jawline. "For years she said she'd never move back here."

He raised an eyebrow. "She hasn't told you why she changed her mind?"

"Nope, and she hasn't told my parents or Doris, either."

"What about Kate?"

He chuckled. "I can't ask my wife to break the best-friend code of confidentiality, but I do know Kate is as puzzled as the rest of us. Apparently my sister usually tells Kate everything."

He narrowed his eyes. "I guess she's looking forward to becoming an aunt when the baby arrives."

"Yes, but even so, this decision is out of character for Megan." Jack frowned. "I wouldn't count on her wanting to stay longer than a year."

Luke nodded, the implicit warning in Jack's tone lodging like a boulder in his heart. It was likely Megan would never be ready to settle down, and he'd be foolish to contemplate the idea of a serious relationship with her again. If her own family doubted her ability to commit to living in Snowgum Creek long-term, he couldn't see her signing an extension on her current contract.

Three days later, Megan stifled a yawn and stood with the Snowgum Creek Community Church congregation for the opening song. She had dragged herself out of bed that morning, determined to make it to church on time. Jack and Kate had given her a lift. They had selected seats in the second-back row, providing an uninterrupted view of the whole building.

Memories of sitting with Luke in this church filled her mind. She scanned the rows on both sides of the center aisle, unable to see him. The music and words on the overhead screen at the front were unfamiliar, and she gave up trying to look as though she was singing along with the congregation.

The song ended and she sat down, a smile curving up her lips. Luke had slipped into a spare seat five rows in front of her across the aisle.

She wriggled in the uncomfortable wooden pew, frustrated that she'd forgotten to collect a cushion when they'd arrived. The muscles in her back and shoulders ached from six days in the orchards, although she had only worked half days toward the end of the week so she could spend more time with Kate.

She opened a Bible that was stashed on a shelf behind the seat in front of her and located the first chapter of Jonah for the first reading. She had discovered her dog-eared Bible from her university days while cleaning up her bedroom. A present from Luke for her eighteenth birthday, he had written a heartfelt and loving message on the inside front cover.

Moisture had filled her eyes as she recalled Luke's generosity and genuine affection. At the tender age of twenty-one and with big dreams for her future, she hadn't realized the gravity of casting aside his love in her pursuit of new adventures.

In the following years she hadn't met a man who measured up to Luke. She valued her friendship with Kate because the social circles she moved in in the city were filled with pleasure-seeking people who lived only for the moment.

Before long the pastor commenced his sermon, talking about how Jonah had run away from the Lord because he didn't want to preach against the wicked citizens in Ninevah.

Megan understood running away. She'd fallen into a pattern of avoiding difficult situations. The Lord had held Jonah to account by creating a wild storm that threatened to destroy the ship he'd boarded, a ship that was headed in the opposite direction away from Ninevah.

She cringed as the pastor spoke his closing words. Jonah knew his actions were the cause of the storm. He had volunteered to be cast overboard and was swallowed by a big fish. Could she escape her past? Was she going to have to face the consequences of her decisions soon?

The service ended and Jack moved away toward the aisle.

Kate stayed in her seat, furrowing her brow. "Meg, please don't be mad with me."

"What's wrong?"

Kate lowered her voice, moving her head closer. "You know how I mentioned we're going out to lunch after church."

She nodded. Jack wanted to buy her lunch to thank her for her work in the orchards. Not that he needed to, because she was a part owner with him and their parents. Her income from the orchards helped finance her overseas trips.

"Um, I kind of forgot to tell you all the details."

"No big deal. Jack mentioned he'd made a booking at the Italian restaurant."

"Did he tell you who else is coming?"

She shook her head, her stomach plummeting like a roller coaster. "You invited Luke?"

"I'm sorry. Jack asked me yesterday to tell you about the change in plans and I totally forgot." She let out a big sigh, her hand resting on her belly. "This pregnancy is causing me to forget everything."

"Is it just the four of us?"

"Yes, and I hope you know we're not trying to set you up with Luke."

"It's okay." She gave her best friend a hug. "Lunch will be fun, and I doubt Luke will think you're trying to match-make."

A petite blonde woman ducked into the row in front of them. She greeted Kate before giving Megan a bright smile. "Megan, you're looking fabulous."

"Amy, wow, it's been a long time. You're looking great." Megan stood. "Congratulations on your marriage."

"Thanks. I'm glad to hear you're staying because I need a good trainer to help me get in shape. Ben's delicious cooking will start piling on the pounds if I don't do something soon."

Luke appeared beside Amy, shooting her a cheeky smile. "Are you criticizing my brother's cooking?"

Amy's blue eyes twinkled. "Of course not, but he likes using ingredients laden with calories. And he burns more calories in the orchard than I do as your clinic nurse." She turned to Megan. "It's great to hear you might be joining us soon."

Megan nodded. "I have a few things to organize first." Her business advisor had confirmed late on Friday afternoon that Luke's contract was a fair deal. Once she checked out the premises, she was prepared to sign the contract.

"And Luke said you may be interested in the cottage."

"Yes, I'm looking for a twelve-month lease."

Amy's face lit her, her smile contagious. "That could work for me."

"Okay, let me know when it's ready to inspect."

"It's ready to go. Ben and I are driving over to Sunny Ridge now to visit family, otherwise I could have shown you today."

"No worries," Megan said. "We can arrange a time later."

Luke turned to Amy. "I can swing by with Megan today and return the keys to you tomorrow at work."

"Good idea." Amy searched her purse and handed Luke a set of keys. "I'd better go and find Ben, otherwise we'll be late. Thanks for helping me out."

"No problem." He slipped the keys into his pocket.

Megan smiled. "Thanks, Amy. I appreciate your help."

"You're welcome. We can talk more during the week." Amy waved goodbye before rushing off toward the front exit.

Kate nudged Megan's forearm, her eyes glittering in the muted light. "Jack said he'd meet us in the hall for coffee. Or would you two prefer to check out the cottage now and meet us at the restaurant?"

Luke shrugged. "I don't mind either way."

Megan held his direct gaze, recognizing an opportunity to delay being interrogated by the townsfolk during morning refreshments. Her mother had forewarned her to expect a couple of people to question her choice to remain single at the age of twenty-nine. "Let's go there first."

"Sure." He smiled. "What time is the lunch booking?"

"Midday," Kate said.

His eyes softened, reminding Megan of molten honey.

"We'll have plenty of time to look at the cottage," he said.

She nodded. "I'll need a lift."

"Okay." He glanced at his watch. "I have to give something to my sister first, and she should be in the hall cleaning up after the children's program."

"That's fine," Megan said.

"We can meet at my Jeep in the back parking lot?"

"Sure." She slung her purse over her shoulder. "See you soon."

Luke joined the queue of parishioners walking toward the side door leading to the hall.

Kate stifled a giggle. "Well, you can't blame me for this one. I thought you were planning to avoid spending extra time with him."

"I'd rather avoid the gossips more, and I do need to find somewhere to live soon."

"I'll miss you if you move into town."

"If I stay at home too long, my mother will drive me crazy. I don't know how you and Jack coped while waiting for your house to be built."

Kate smiled. "Your parents traveled around Australia for nearly a year after our wedding."

"True. That does make a difference."

"You know, I'm pleased you and Luke are friends."

She nodded. It seemed as though she couldn't avoid seeing Luke. If only he didn't still inspire feelings in her that she'd rather ignore.

Chapter 3

Luke unlocked his Jeep and glanced around the parking lot. Megan walked toward him, long dark hair flowing down her back and knee-length dress swirling around her legs.

He drew in a deep breath, marveling again at her beauty. Old feelings resurfaced and he squashed them down, intent on extinguishing the power she still commanded over his thoughts and feelings.

His sister had forgotten her house keys, and he'd given Rachel his keys rather than meeting her after church at their home. He didn't intend to let Rachel know he was having lunch with Megan.

He rolled his shoulders, releasing a tension knot in his back. Speculation within his family regarding the state of his relationship with Megan was already too intense for his liking.

A brilliant smile covered Megan's face as she approached him. "Thanks for volunteering to show me the cottage."

"No problem. I know Amy and Ben are really busy until they finish apple picking." He opened the passenger door and she stepped up into the leather seat.

He made his way around to the driver's side and switched on the engine.

She relaxed into her seat. "Which street is Amy's cottage on?"

"Berkley, around the corner from the clinic and two blocks from the hospital."

"Sounds perfect. And the health club is in walking distance, too."

He nodded, reversing out of the parking spot. "It's a convenient location in a nice neighborhood you probably won't recognize since many of the homes have been renovated."

She smoothed her skirt over her knees and looked at the passing landscape.

They turned onto Berkley, and he parked in front of a quaint English-style cottage.

He cast a critical eye over the garden and small patch of lawn. A dozen rosebushes bloomed behind the white picket fence. The cottage was in immaculate condition, and he understood why Amy had liked living there.

Megan walked along the path leading to the house. "The garden is pretty."

He nodded. "The roses require a little bit of attention, otherwise it's easy to look after."

She paused, inhaling the scent of a scarlet rose. "I don't mind gardening, although it's not something I've done for many years."

"Did you live in an apartment in Sydney?"

"Yes, not that I was home very much." She spun around and met his gaze. "I paid my share of the rent all year round and used it as a base."

"Are you keeping the Sydney apartment?"

She shook her head. "I boxed up all my belongings before I left, and they're ready to be transported here."

He raised an eyebrow and strolled beside her to the front entrance of the cottage. "You were confident you'd stay in Snowgum Creek?"

She nodded. "I'd already decided that I wanted the hospital job, and I also had the option of staying with Mom and Dad if I couldn't pick up extra work to supplement my income."

His professional respect for her increased by a couple of notches. He couldn't deny he was intrigued to learn she'd been prepared to commit to living in Snowgum Creek without the added benefit of leasing a room in his clinic. Maybe he'd underestimated her.

He unlocked the front door and strode inside, pointing out rooms and commenting on the layout.

"Wow, this space is very functional." She walked over to the large windows overlooking the private backyard.

"There's a bit of lawn to mow."

"That's okay. I can borrow my dad's mower."

"A good idea. Rachel and I also have one you could borrow." He smiled, picturing Megan pushing a mower around the yard without any trouble or raising a sweat. Her fitness level was phenomenal, and left him behind in the breeze. "Overall, the gardens are fairly low maintenance."

She nodded. "You sound like a Realtor."

He laughed. "My little brother must have taught me a few tricks."

"Speaking of Caleb, what's he doing these days?"

"Real estate in Sunny Ridge."

"I can see him doing well in that job." She walked through the kitchen, opening cupboards, checking out the oven and dishwasher. "Everything looks good. I'll contact Amy tomorrow."

"Do you want to look at the backyard?"

She shook her head. "I've seen enough. Can we make a time this week to look at the consulting room in your clinic?"

"Sure. I've no idea what my schedule is like, and I also have a couple of extra shifts at the hospital to cover."

"You sound crazy busy."

"This is normal."

Her eyes widened. "Really?"

"Yep. It's probably easier to call my receptionist and book a half-hour slot at your convenience."

"Sounds like a plan."

His phone beeped and he grabbed it from his pocket, reading the brief message from the on-call doctor at Snowgum Creek Hospital.

"Is everything okay?"

"I may need to stop by the hospital a bit later." He glanced at the time on his phone. "We probably should head over to the restaurant."

She nodded. "Did you know I was invited to lunch?"

"To be honest, I can't remember if Jack mentioned it." He rubbed his hand over the back of his neck, fatigue assaulting his muscles. "I did a late shift at the hospital Friday night, and I wasn't really awake when Jack called me yesterday morning."

She twisted the strap of her purse around her fingers. "Kate was worried we'd think they were trying to set us up."

He chuckled, having endured a number of setups from well-meaning friends and relatives in recent years. "We'll be working together, and it's inevitable we'll run into each other socially."

"True."

He held her gaze, mesmerized by the warmth emanating from her gorgeous blue eyes. "I'd like to think we can still be friends."

"Yes, me, too." She scraped her teeth over her lower

lip. "I know I was immature years ago, and I could have handled things differently."

He nodded. "We were both young."

She blinked, a sheen of moisture filling her eyes. "I'm sorry I ran away and hurt you."

He gulped in a shallow breath, having not expected to receive an apology. "It's not all your fault, and I should have known you weren't ready to get married."

"My mother despairs that I'll never be ready to settle down."

"At least Jack is providing a grandchild, and a welcome distraction that will take some of the pressure off."

"Very true." She relaxed her mouth into a slight smile. "Thanks for being understanding."

He nodded, remembering how much he had missed their friendship. If he kept his focus on their professional relationship, he might survive the next twelve months with his heart intact.

Two days later, Megan walked along the short path leading to the front entrance of the Snowgum Creek Medical Clinic. Luke's contract was folded up in her purse, and she was ready to sign it today if the consulting room met her specifications.

She pushed open the door and walked into the waiting room.

An older woman who looked vaguely familiar smiled and greeted her by name from behind the reception desk. "Luke said he'll be ready to see you in a few minutes. He suggested you go ahead and check out the room." She pointed to a closed door on the far side of the waiting room.

"Thanks." She crossed the room and opened the door. A modern desk dominated the far corner, and three leather chairs were arranged around the desk. A row of cupboards ran along one wall, with counter space on top and a sink at one end. The carpeted floor and paintwork looked brand-new, the muted shades of blue creating a professional and friendly atmosphere.

Luke appeared in the doorway. "What do you think?"

She smiled. "The leather seats are a nice touch."

"I did have a doctor from Sunny Ridge using this room but he retired a few months ago. We also have a staff room with a kitchen attached. Would you like a cup of tea or coffee?"

"Coffee would be great."

"Okay, I'll show you the kitchen."

She followed Luke to the reception desk, where he introduced her to his receptionist, Janice, before leading Megan to the staff room. They entered a large room, a long table on one side and a full-size kitchen on the other.

An expensive coffee machine sat on the kitchen counter.

She lifted a brow. "I'm impressed, and I'll be tempted to drop in every day for coffee."

"Amy makes the best coffee out of everyone here. My barista skills need work, and unfortunately Amy isn't here this afternoon."

"I once worked in a café in Italy, although I haven't used one of these machines in ages."

His smile widened. "You're more than welcome to have a go now. No doubt you'll do a much better job than me. I'm just a doctor."

She placed her purse on the counter and inspected the machine. Luke fetched a container of ground coffee and a carton of milk. She set to work, percolating the coffee and frothing the milk. "Cappuccino or latte?"

"Latte, please."

She found coffee mugs in an overhead cupboard and

made two lattes, swirling the froth into a spiral pattern. "Should I make one for Janice?"

He shook his head. "She only drinks English breakfast tea and has a fresh cup on her desk."

They carried their lattes back to Megan's new room. She sank into the soft leather chair behind the glass-topped desk. "I could sit here drinking coffee all day."

"Couldn't we all. Do you have any questions about the contract?"

"No." Her business advisor had mentioned that the financial penalty for breaking the contract was steeper than industry standard. A frustrating minor detail, but she understood Luke's need to protect his business interests and why he believed she was a flight risk. A belief she was determined to dispel over the coming months by proving she could fulfill her twelve-month contractual obligations.

She inhaled the aromatic brew before taking a sip. "Not bad for my first attempt."

"It tastes great."

"I'll get better with practice." She rifled through the junk in her purse, locating a pen and the envelope containing the contract. She flattened out the folded sheets of paper on the desk. "I'll sign it for you now."

"Are you a hundred percent sure this is what you want to do?"

She sucked in a deep breath. "Okay, I'm going to tell you something and you must promise not to tell anyone, especially Jack."

He nodded. "You have my word. What's wrong?"

"There is a reason why I'm not going back to the ski resort this year."

"Did something happen?"

"That's the problem. I can't prove it but my instincts are usually right."

He frowned. "Megan, you're worrying me. What's going on?"

"It's a long story, and I'll try to give you the short version." She flicked the pen between her fingers. "There's this guy who started working at the resort two seasons ago. Last year things got a little intense."

"Was he your boyfriend?"

She shook her head. "He did ask me out ages ago but I declined. I thought I'd made it clear that I wasn't interested."

"But he didn't take no for an answer."

"Not exactly. He never said or did anything inappropriate, but as the season progressed he was always hanging around wherever I was."

"At work or socially?"

"Both. You have to remember the resort village is like a small community and we all tend to hang out together outside of work hours." She dropped her gaze and sipped her coffee. "He's also a ski instructor, and he changed his roster to coincide with my work hours. He always attended the weekly gym class I instructed, and he seemed to be around wherever I turned."

"Did you make a complaint?"

"And say what?" She pressed her fingertips to her forehead, feeling the tension forming in her head. "I figured if I took a break from the resort for at least one season, he'd either forget about me or find someone else to obsess over."

He drained his coffee mug and placed it on her desk. "You could have a lodged a complaint with the police."

"Would they believe me? My friends in the village joked about how he was always around, but I got the impression they thought he was harmless." She tucked her hair back behind her ears. "And what if I was wrong? I didn't want to ruin his reputation by overreacting to the situation."

"He could be unbalanced. What's his name? How old is he?"

"Jason, and he's about twenty-five, maybe younger." She sighed. "I don't want you to make this into a big deal."

"It's obviously a big deal to you, otherwise you'd be working at the ski village this year."

"Maybe not. Jack and Kate's baby is a pretty good incentive to stay here." She smiled.

"Have you told anyone else about this guy?"

She lowered her lashes. "No. I'm only telling you so you'll understand why I'm committed to staying in Snowgum Creek. I don't want you to overreact—"

"It sounds like harassment to me. I'm not overreacting when I say that bullying and harassment are a real problem in the workplace." He rubbed his hand over his jaw, his brows drawn together. "I've seen it before, and I have zero tolerance for this kind of behavior."

"I just want to forget about it."

"Did you confront this guy and make it clear you wanted him to stay away?"

She shook her head. "I didn't have any concrete evidence, and it could have all been a coincidence."

"Not likely." A steely tone entered his voice. "If you hear from this guy, I want you to promise me that you'll do something about it."

"Okay. I'm not planning to go to the ski resort this season, and it's very unlikely I'll see him here."

He narrowed his eyes. "If you do see him in Snowgum Creek, then you'll know you have a problem you need to address."

She flicked through the documents and signed the agreement. "Here you go. Let's forget about him and talk about something more positive."

He nodded. "Congratulations on your new business venture."

"Thank you." She finished her latte and lounged back in her chair, confident the problems with Jason were in the past. And confident she could build a working relationship with Luke. She had squandered her opportunity to have a relationship with him, and any thoughts in that direction were futile.

Chapter 4

Luke gripped the edge of the counter in front of the coffeemaker, resisting the urge to thump the confounded machine. Why had he let Amy talk him into buying it?

Megan strolled into the staff room. "Is everything okay?"

He frowned. "The machine won't work."

"Really?" She picked up a coffee mug from the shelf. "Is it broken?"

"Not exactly. Amy usually makes my latte."

Her lips curved into a smile. "Where is Amy?"

"At a school assembly for my niece, and my next patient arrives in ten minutes."

"I'm totally shocked that I can do something you can't do."

"Yeah, why don't you rub it in and make me beg."

Her wide smile highlighted a dimple on her cheek. "Okay, I'll make your latte for you."

The hint of mischief in her tone lightened his mood. "Thanks, I owe you."

"You do know there's instant coffee in the cupboard?"

He nodded. "I used to happily drink instant until my sister-in-law converted me to the superior flavor of coffee from this wretched machine."

She chuckled. "How do you cope when Amy's not here?"

"I call in my order and collect it from the café up the road."

"Wow, I didn't know you'd become a coffee snob."

He rolled his eyes. "By accident rather than choice."

"Yeah, right." She set to work brewing two coffees.

He rested his hand on the counter beside her. "How are you settling in? Do you have many appointments booked?"

"Yes, I have a number of clients booked in through the business, and my calendar is full for the next two months at the hospital."

"That's great news." He hoped her hospital position would be ongoing.

"It's good for the community." She spooned milky froth onto their lattes and handed him a mug. "Enjoy."

"Thanks." He sat next to her at the table and added a generous spoonful of sugar, the fine granules sinking into the milky mixture. Janice had brought in a container of homemade chocolate cookies and he offered one to Megan.

She shook her head. "I'm not hungry."

"You'll offend Janice if you don't eat her cookies." He popped the smallest one from the container into his mouth, savoring the sweet flavor.

"You'll have to eat my share."

"All right." He sipped his latte. "Have you seen or heard from that guy?"

Her eyes widened. "Nope, but I don't think he'll bother me."

"I wouldn't count on it."

She lifted a brow. "Why? I could be overreacting to the whole situation."

"Or your instincts could be right." Emily, his longtime friend from med school, had moved to Sunny Ridge Hospital from Sydney a few years ago due to a harassment issue. The perpetrator had followed her to Sunny Ridge, and a nasty confrontation involving the police ensued. After witnessing Emily's angst, he couldn't brush aside Megan's valid concerns. He just wished she'd take it seriously.

She lounged back in her seat. "I think you're worrying for nothing."

"Maybe. This is good coffee, but don't tell Amy I said so."

"Don't tell me what?" Amy breezed into the room, her long blond ponytail swaying behind her.

"Nothing important. Megan knows how to use your machine."

Amy glanced at her watch. "I'm sorry I'm late back. The assembly ran overtime, but you'd be so proud of your niece. Chloe played the piano beautifully while her class sang along."

"I'm glad to hear it went well."

Megan asked, "Has she been playing for long?"

Amy shook her head. "I started teaching her last year and she has talent."

"Yes, she's making excellent progress." He drank the remainder of his coffee. "I need to get back to work since my next patient is due any minute."

Amy frowned. "Luke, you really are working too hard. I thought you'd scheduled a half-hour gap this morning."

"A couple of patients ran late, and another patient needed to come in now instead of later this afternoon." He turned to Megan. "Thanks for the coffee."

"You're welcome. Amy, would you like one?"

"Sounds great." She rummaged in her purse. "Found it." She handed a set of keys to Megan. "For the cottage. I know you're not officially moving in for a few weeks, but Ben and I have cleared out all my stuff. You can start moving in whenever you're ready."

"Thanks. That will be helpful."

Amy nodded. "It'll be good when you're settled. I hate that living-in-limbo feeling."

Luke stood. "I guess Megan is used to it."

Megan shrugged. "It will be nice to settle here for a while."

"You mean a year," he said.

"Who knows?" She flicked her hair back off her face. "I might stay longer."

He rinsed his coffee mug in the sink, refusing to respond to her flippant comment. He doubted her ability to curtail her long-held wanderlust tendencies. What would it take to inspire Megan to live in Snowgum Creek long-term?

Megan adjusted the settings on a stationary bike in the Snowgum Creek Health Club. The cycle class was due to start in five minutes, and there were only two bikes remaining for latecomers. She tucked her hoodie into her gym bag, and threw a towel over the bike handlebars. Her large bottle of chilled water, stashed in a holder, would keep her hydrated through the forty-five-minute class.

She settled on the bike, her legs falling into the familiar routine. This was her favorite class to attend and teach. She turned the bike pedal tension up a few notches as her muscles started to warm up. Her heart rate monitor watch synced with the bike's settings, and she let out a few deep breaths. After a busy day at Snowgum Creek Hospital, she needed an outlet to release all her stress and tension.

"Megan."

Luke's deep voice spiked her heart rate and she turned to face him. "Hey."

He placed his towel on the spare bike beside her in the back row. "I didn't know you attended this class."

"I didn't make it to the gym this morning, and the time suits me today."

He lifted the stem of his bike seat, raising the height. "How often do you train?"

"At least five days a week, sometimes more. Some days are lighter than others."

"I try to train three times a week." He jumped on the bike, his T-shirt and loose-fitting shorts highlighting his lean and muscular build.

She swallowed hard, switching her attention to the front of the room. The instructor spoke into his microphone and ramped up the music volume. Megan wore her usual Lycra combo of a fitted top and knee-length bike pants. Her cycling shoes were clipped into the pedals.

Perspiration cooled her body as the workout grew more intense. Fans circulated air around the steamy room. She focused her attention on her cycling speed and technique, enjoying the rush of endorphins that kicked in when she trained at maximum capacity.

She drank from her water bottle, sneaking another glance in Luke's direction at the end of the fourth track. Drenched in sweat, his breathing was fast from pushing himself hard during the class.

He smiled. "How you doing?"

"Pretty good."

"How's your calorie count going?"

"I'm tracking well." Her heart rate monitor provided a reasonably accurate reading.

He wiped his towel over his face. "My bike is picking up your heart rate."

"Then you'll know how hard I'm working out."

He grinned. "Do you think you're working harder than me?"

She shrugged. "I'm pushing the high gears on the hills."

"Me, too."

The next song started and she refocused. The instructor provided clear instructions, cueing the class on what was coming up next. This track had a long hill climb followed by a downhill sprint. She closed her eyes and stood, imagining she was outdoors and climbing a steep hill on a winding mountain road. She increased the bike tension, her muscles burning as she pushed through the tough climb.

The pinnacle of the hill reached, she dropped to her seat and flew into a downhill sprint. She lowered the bike tension and pedaled fast. Luke stayed in sync with her, his legs rocketing through the sprint phase. Maybe he was fit enough to keep up with her blistering pace.

The track ended and she sucked in a few deep breaths, her lungs screaming for more oxygen. She grabbed her bottle. Her parched throat appreciated the refreshing cool water.

She met Luke's amused gaze.

His breathing was ragged. "I can keep up with you."

She smiled. "Maybe."

The rest of the class passed in a blur of frantic activity, and Megan lowered the bike tension during the cooldown track. She released the remaining tightness in her muscles during the stretches at the end.

She rubbed her towel over her damp skin, her cycling clothes moist from perspiration. Luke passed her a few sheets of paper towel and cleaning spray.

"Thanks." She wiped down the bike and slipped on her hoodie. Her plan was to drive home to the farm and jump straight into a hot shower.

"What are you doing tonight?" Luke asked.

She paused. Where was this heading? "Going home.

Mom has put aside dinner to reheat in the microwave and then it's early to bed for me."

"You have an early start?"

She nodded and sat on the carpeted floor behind her bike, leaning back against the wall. "I'm meeting a client here at five-thirty." She pulled off her cycling shoes. "What are you doing tonight?"

"I'm on call at the hospital from eight to midnight."

"Are you looking for company, or someone to cook you dinner?"

"Both." He grinned. "Rach is out tonight and spaghetti on toast gets boring."

She tied up the laces on her sneakers. "Cook an egg as well, or open a tin of baked beans instead of spaghetti. The protein boost will do you good after your workout."

"Okay, boss."

She laughed. "You'll cope." She stood and waved goodnight to the instructor before heading out of the gym with Luke. "By the way, I was impressed by your fitness."

"I train outdoors when I can. I like to do a couple of early-morning rides, work schedule and weather permitting."

"Really?" She paused, holding his gaze. "I was thinking about doing a few training rides in the mountains."

"You shouldn't do them alone because the phone reception is sketchy."

"True." She nibbled on her lower lip. "I'll have to come up with another plan."

"Why don't we start training together?" His eyes sparkled. "I'm probably one of the few people in town who could keep up with your cracking pace."

She nodded. "Sounds good, as long as you're up for the challenge. I'll push you hard."

He laughed. "I won't knock free personal training. We

can always loop around town. The cycle paths have been improved in recent years, and you can do a five-mile circuit, including a few hills, off-road."

"Okay, it's a deal. We'll compare schedules and see what we can work out."

"Great. By the way, I'm free to help you move in a few weeks if you're still looking for people. It was Saturday afternoon, right?"

"Yes, and thank you. I appreciate your help." Between Jack and Luke, she could complete the move from the farm in a couple of trips. Her mother was delighted that she was finally shifting the furniture and personal effects she'd been storing for years at the farm. She'd booked a delivery truck to move her furniture from Sydney to the cottage.

They reached his Jeep in the parking lot, and he beeped open the lock. "I'll see you tomorrow."

She waved goodbye and headed over to her car. The late-model hatchback served her well as she clocked up the miles commuting to Sunny Ridge once a week.

Luke drove out of the parking lot, and his taillights disappeared into the distance. She'd fallen back into a comfortable friendship with him that hadn't really been challenged until tonight. The old attraction was still there, and she did her best to squash long-dormant feelings.

She could maintain a friendship and keep her heart intact. He may have forgiven her for running out on him years ago, but she was under no illusion that he wanted to revive their previous relationship. She didn't deserve a second chance.

Luke sat cross-legged on the floor in the middle of Megan's spacious new bedroom, reading the bed assembly instructions. Jack had left a few minutes earlier, the last of the boxes and furniture now stowed in Megan's cottage.

She stood in the doorway and he looked up, meeting her gaze. "You've purchased a complicated bed to build."

She placed her hands on her slim hips, her sweatshirt and long black pants marked with dust. "I can worry about it tomorrow."

"You should sleep in your new bed tonight." She'd spent hours unpacking while he helped Jack move all her gear from the farm.

"I know, but the sofa is kind of comfortable, if you curl up the right way."

"I can build the bed but I'll need your help to put the wooden frame together."

"Sure. I appreciate your help with the move. Thank you."

"You're welcome."

"Are you on call at the hospital tonight?"

"From seven. I need to call in around nine and check up on a couple of patients. Hopefully I'll have a quiet night."

"Do you have dinner plans?"

He grinned. "Are you offering?"

"The least I can do is feed you, after you've slaved away helping me move." The golden light slicing through the window cast a soft glow over her beautiful face.

His heart skipped a beat. How could he resist her offer? "Are you set up to cook?"

She nodded. "The kitchen is nearly unpacked, and the fridge and pantry are stocked. I bought food yesterday."

"You are organized. What's on the menu?"

"Pumpkin risotto."

"Sounds great." He'd figured she'd cook healthy.

"I'll make a start on the risotto now, and be back soon to help with the bed."

"No worries."

Luke made quick progress, and the frame was ready to assemble when she returned. He lined up a row of wooden slats. "If you can hold the end of the bed upright, I'll slide in the slats and attach the bed head."

"Sure."

She followed his directions, and within ten minutes they had placed the mattress on the bed frame. "It'll be nice to sleep in a comfortable bed."

He pointed to a dining chair in the corner with her quilt and two pillows on it. "Your mother brought over freshly laundered bed linen."

"Did she ask you to assemble my bed?"

He shook his head. "She asked Jack, but he ran out of time."

She sighed. "I'm so looking forward to having my own space."

"Are you feeling henpecked?"

"I shouldn't complain. My mom has good intentions, and she's very excited that I'm living close by for the first time in years."

"My mom has good intentions, too. Plus she feeds me on a regular basis without complaining."

"What's the catch?"

He groaned. "She tells me I need to find a wife to look after me."

She giggled. "Apparently I need a husband and children, too."

"Ben and Amy are at my folks' for dinner tonight."

"Are you supposed to be there?"

He shrugged. "I sometimes turn up at the last minute so that my mother can't make any plans to invite unexpected guests."

"Unexpected single female guests?"

"Yep, you got it."

"Oh, no, does she try to do this often?"

"Not if I can help it. She seems to forget I'm a busy doctor with a crazy schedule and not much time for a social life."

"My mom is excited I'm staying in one place for a year. She sees that as progress."

He stood. "Are you going to teach me how to make risotto?"

She drew her brows together. "I've heard about your cooking abilities."

"Really?" He followed her into the kitchen. "I'm willing to learn."

She added a portion of butter to the fry pan. "Risotto is not the kind of dish where you can just throw in all the ingredients and hope for the best. There's technique involved in reducing the stock during the cooking process."

He crossed his arms over his chest. "Well, if you're not going to teach me, I may land on your doorstep for dinner again."

She laughed. "I'm onto you. How many friends do you visit for dinner?"

He widened his eyes. "They all feel sorry for the overworked doctor."

"I'm sure they do. Especially the single female ones."

His phone chimed—a call from the hospital. "I'll be back in a minute."

Megan focused her attention on the risotto, aware Luke stood only inches behind her, peering over her shoulder. His expensive aftershave mingled with the pumpkin-and-onion aroma, a pleasant combination.

Her pulse kicked up a notch. She liked having him close by in her kitchen. This picture of domestic bliss had haunted her dreams after she'd left him. She sucked in a steadying breath. They were friends, nothing more. According to Amy, Luke had a number of female friends. She was part of the crowd, no one special. She'd thrown away that privilege years ago.

He took a step back. "Would you like me to set the table?"

"Yes, please. You may need to clear some junk off it."

"Sure." He located cutlery and two plates. "What would you like to drink?"

"There's water in the fridge."

He left the kitchen and she stirred the risotto. It would be ready to serve in two minutes. She found a large ceramic bowl and scooped the steaming risotto out of the fry pan and into the bowl. Luke had laid out two place settings, and she placed the bowl in the center of the round table.

He walked into the living room, his smile widening. "Wow, the risotto smells good."

"I hope you like it."

He sat beside her. "Can I say grace?"

"Sure." She'd fallen out of the habit of saying grace before meals.

He closed his eyes and reached for her hand.

His grip was firm and comforting. She followed his lead and let out a deep breath.

"Lord, thank You for this wonderful food and company. Amen."

"Amen." She opened her eyes, captivated by his warm gaze.

He sampled the risotto. "This is excellent."

"Thanks." She tasted a spoonful, appreciating the delicate flavors. The rice was cooked to perfection, with just the right consistency and texture.

His phone beeped and he frowned.

"The hospital?"

"Probably." He retrieved his phone from his pocket and read the message on the screen.

"Do you need to leave now?"

"No, I have fifteen minutes. There has been a bad car accident an hour out of town. A tourist has hit a roo."

"Oh, no, are they okay?"

"The call just came in. An ambulance is heading to the scene and I need to be at the hospital right at seven." He ate a mouthful of risotto.

"It sounds like you're in for a long night."

He nodded. "Thanks for dinner. This will keep me going, and I'm glad we ate early."

"Me, too."

"Are you going to church tomorrow?"

"Maybe, although I was thinking about sleeping in."

"Why don't you come to the night service?"

She arched a brow. "I haven't been to the evening service in years."

"It's a youth service but I quite like it. The service starts at seven."

"Okay, I'll think about it."

He stood. "I'm sorry I have to run out on you and can't stay to help with the dishes."

"No problem. You did spend all afternoon moving my stuff." She followed him to the front door and switched on the outside light. "I hope you have a chance to sleep tonight."

He slipped on his jacket. "We'll see. I may end up sleeping the day away tomorrow."

"Take care."

He walked to his Jeep and she stood in the doorway, wrapping her arms around her body as a blast of cold air hit her from outside. He was right. His life was unpredictable, and he couldn't make definite plans if he was on call.

She whispered a brief prayer for the occupants of the car. She hoped and prayed Luke wouldn't have to deal with a tragedy tonight.

Chapter 5

Luke stifled a yawn and slid into an aisle seat toward the back of Snowgum Creek Community Church. After a long night at the hospital, he'd slept late this morning before heading out for a ninety-minute bike ride around town. He'd needed the fresh air and stress release provided by the arduous course he'd chosen to ride.

He glanced around the building as it filled with teens and young adults. Would Megan turn up tonight? The service started in five minutes.

He shook his head, thoughts of Megan refusing to shift out of his mind. Yesterday and last night had been like old times. Their resurrected lighthearted friendship had ignited a yearning for more. A yearning he must deny, knowing her time in Snowgum Creek was only temporary. In less than twelve months, she'd leave town without a backward glance. This time he wouldn't allow her departure to shatter his heart.

The band stopped playing, and the service leader took hold of the microphone. After a brief introduction, the congregation stood for the first song.

Megan appeared beside him halfway through the song, and he shuffled over to make room for her next to him.

"Sorry I'm late," she whispered.

"I'd wondered if you were still coming."

"I was held up at the farm." She draped her elegant full-length woolen coat over the back of the pew. "I stopped by this afternoon to collect a few things, and Mom didn't want me to leave."

"She's missing you already?"

She nodded. "Crazy, huh?"

The song ended and he sat, shifting on the hard seat to find a more comfortable position.

Megan's sweet perfume tantalized his senses, and his awareness of her, only inches away, intensified. He kept his gaze fixed on the service leader, trying to ignore the beautiful woman by his side.

Who was he kidding? He hadn't been able to resist her charms years ago, and nothing had changed. He sucked in a steadying breath. He was an adult, a doctor and capable of controlling all of his emotional responses.

She stood with him for the second song, and she didn't attempt to sing along. His curiosity was piqued. Why had she walked away from the church after being fervent about her faith in her youth? Another question lingered in his mind. Why had she chosen to come along tonight? Was she seeking to renew her faith and reconnect with God?

Lord, You know Megan's heart. Please draw her closer to You and strengthen her as she faces the challenges of life.

He tried to block out Megan's intoxicating presence and focus on the sermon. Maybe staying for dinner at her place last night had been a mistake. Had he crossed a line that was better left alone? Or was fatigue the problem? If he wasn't so exhausted, maybe he'd have a tighter grip on his emotions.

The service passed quickly, and before long they were singing the final song. He glanced at Megan. She seemed relaxed and more at ease than at the start of the service.

The song ended and she perched on the edge of her seat, reaching for her coat.

He dropped down beside her. "What did you think?"

"The service is more modern than I remember."

"Yes, it's very contemporary, which appeals to the youth."

"Did you have a rough night?"

He nodded. "I went to bed around four and woke at midday."

She frowned. "Were the people in the car okay?"

"We transported one patient to the spinal unit at Sunny Ridge, and the other two with less serious injuries stayed with us."

"I'm glad there were no fatalities."

"Me, too." A late-night brawl outside the local pub had delayed him leaving the hospital by a few hours. The injured men were known troublemakers from out of town, and the police were called in to deal with them.

Kara, an old school friend and coleader of the church youth group, caught his eye. He waved to her as she headed over in his direction.

Megan followed his gaze, her eyes darkening. "She looks familiar. Do I know her?"

"You don't remember Kara from school?"

"Oh, yes, I do now."

Megan plastered a smile on her face. How could she forget Kara?

Kara beamed a bright smile at Luke. "Hey, I was hoping to catch up with you before you left."

Luke smiled. "Do you remember Megan?"

"Of course." Kara's smile wavered. "Long time no see."

"Yes, you're looking well." Kara hadn't changed much since high school. Long, mousy-colored hair, wire-rimmed glasses and conservative clothing more suited to her mother's generation. And never-ending devotion to Luke.

"Thanks. Um, I heard you'd moved back to town. Are you staying long?"

"At least a year." She tossed her long glossy hair back over her shoulders, glad she'd taken the time to apply more makeup than her usual mascara and lipstick. "It's a nice change from traveling all the time."

Luke gave Kara an indulgent smile that set Megan's teeth on edge.

"What did you need to talk about?" he asked.

"The upcoming youth group camp. I've made the booking and wanted to confirm the date still worked for you."

He nodded. "I'm organizing Emily, a doctor friend of mine in Sunny Ridge, to cover for me at the clinic."

"Great." Kara's smile broadened, lighting up her face. "I'll get the ball rolling on planning the weekend. We have ten weeks to pull it all together. Can you make it on Friday night?"

"Yes, but I think I'm on call the following week."

"Sure." Kara shifted her uneasy gaze to Megan. "I'll leave you two to chat. Nice to see you again, Megan."

"You, too." She pressed her lips together, disconcerted by the conversation she'd witnessed.

Kara walked away and Luke's frown deepened. "I thought you'd be happy to see Kara again."

"I wasn't unhappy to see her."

"You weren't exactly brimming with enthusiasm, either."

She bristled at the critical tone in his voice. "Have you forgotten? Kara and I weren't exactly close in high school." *Rivals* was a better description because Megan had won the prize: Luke.

"High school was a long time ago."

"I know." It seemed like an eternity since she'd last sat with Luke at an evening service in this church. Life had been much less complicated back then. "I heard you help out with youth group."

He nodded. "I try to attend most Friday nights, depending on work commitments."

"Your job must make it hard."

"Tell me about it."

She stood, her gaze taking in the groups of young people congregating around the building. "I feel too old to be here."

"No way. I often head out for coffee with the youth group, but I need an early night."

"Me, too." The move had exhausted her, and she had a busy week coming up.

"I'm glad Kara was able to book the camp." He stood. "It was the only weekend this year that I could line up Emily as a short-term replacement at the clinic."

She nodded. Kara was going to spend an entire weekend with Luke. Megan tightened her grip on her purse. She had no claim on Luke, no reason for the green-eyed monster to lurk in the dark recesses of her suspicious mind. It was none of her business if Kara wanted to pursue Luke.

Megan lifted her chin, determined to let it go. No good could come from holding a grudge against Kara.

Luke pushed his mountain bike past the squeaky gate and around to the back of Megan's house, ready for their early-morning ride. His feet crunched on dew, the patchy morning frost remaining on the grass shaded by the house.

Megan slouched in a chair on her back deck, slipping on her cycling shoes. Her bike leaned against the balcony railing, and sunlight created streaks of gold on the wooden decking.

He smiled. "Morning, I see you're all set to go."

She stood. "Yes. It's a bit crisp but we'll warm up soon enough."

She wore a purple long-sleeve cycling top and black full-length pants. The windchill could be a problem, and he was glad she was prepared.

"Did you check your bike is up for the challenge?" he asked.

"Not yet. I accidentally slept through my alarm."

"No worries." He squeezed a tire between his fingers. "Do you have a bike pump handy?"

"Isn't it attached to the bike?"

"Nope."

She wrinkled her brow. "I think it's in the garage somewhere."

"I'll pump up your tires with mine."

"Thanks. I'll lock up the house while you do it."

Minutes later she followed him, wheeling her bike around to the front of her house. "Which route are we taking?"

"I thought we could ride a circuit around town. There shouldn't be much traffic at this time of day and there's the steep hill climb to the lookout."

"Sounds good."

They rode single file along the tree-lined streets of Snowgum Creek before reaching the road up to the lookout.

He dropped to a low gear and pushed through the winding climb, his warm muscles feeling the exertion. Megan cruised ahead, taking the steep hill in her stride. He pulled to a stop at the top, a few minutes behind her.

She grinned, her face red and her breathing even. "Did you feel it?"

He nodded, taking a minute to catch his breath. "You made it look easy."

"I push myself hard on the stationary bikes."

"I can tell." His gaze took in the panoramic view of Snowgum Creek and the surrounding district. "I love this view."

"Me, too." Sunglasses shaded her eyes, blocking out the glare from the early-morning rays. "Do you remember when we used to ride up here?"

"How could I forget?" After school they'd race to the top, and then make out on the wooden bench only a few feet away.

She pulled off her bike helmet and slipped her sunglasses on top of her head. "We used to have a lot of fun together."

"Yep, back in the days when I could beat you up the hill."

She laughed. "You weren't far behind me today, and don't forget cycling is part of my job."

He sipped water from his bottle. "We'll have to go for a ride through the pine forest one day and see what your cycling endurance is really like."

"You're on, and I'm confident you won't find me lagging behind." She leaned her bike against the back of the bench, her gaze fixed on the township below. "I haven't been up here in years. Snowgum Creek has grown over the last decade."

He nodded. "A new estate has been built on the eastern side of town overlooking the mountains."

"I can understand why. The view is breathtaking."

He joined her beside the bench, his attention drawn to his half-built house on top of a hill on the edge of town. His first residential property investment, and the fulfillment of a lifelong dream to live and work in Snowgum Creek.

She flipped her ponytail back over her shoulder. "Are you set to stay here indefinitely?"

"Yes, this town is my home." He sucked in a refreshing breath of cold mountain air, knowing she couldn't fathom his attachment to this part of the world. One day he hoped to fill his sprawling new home with children of his own. Megan wasn't the settling-down type who would be content with the small-town life of doctor's wife and mother. Any thoughts in that direction were futile.

Megan tucked her purse under her arm as she walked out of the clinic and into the Saturday-morning sunshine. A cool breeze stirred up the fallen leaves on the path, inspiring her to quicken her pace. The cottage garden at the front of the clinic contained a couple of hardy flowering plants that had survived the midwinter frosts.

She adjusted her soft woolen scarf around her neck. They'd had a few light snow showers this winter, the weather milder than usual. She glanced at her watch, thankful she had time to duck home before meeting Luke for lunch at a café on the main street.

They had arranged a business meeting to discuss how she'd settled into working in the clinic. Luke had referred a number of exercise physiology patients her way, although most of her work was at the hospital.

Luke's work schedule was crazy. They passed each other in the clinic and hospital, but he often didn't have time to stop and chat. Church and their occasional outdoor cycling rides or gym classes were the only opportunities she had to talk with him.

She turned in the direction of her house and a man approached her, sunglasses hiding his eyes.

"Megan."

She froze. No, this couldn't be happening. Jason should be at the ski fields, not in Snowgum Creek!

He stepped out in front of her, blocking her path.

"Megan, it's good to see you."

She cringed. "What are you doing here?"

"It's my weekend off, and I thought I'd take a break, travel around."

Yeah, right. As if that was the real reason he was here. "Why Snowgum Creek?"

"I remembered how you used to talk about your home-town."

"Oh." Her stomach compressed into a tight knot, her gut instincts screaming that she was right.

He didn't seem in a hurry to go anywhere, a wide smile covering his tanned face. How could she get rid of him without causing a scene? This side of the quiet, tree-lined street was deserted, the clinic now closed for the day.

"How come you're not working at the resort this year?" he asked.

She shrugged. "I wanted to do something different, explore other opportunities."

"Why?"

"Because I can."

"Everyone misses you." He shoved his hands in his pockets. "It's not the same without you."

The intensity in his voice drove a shard of fear into her heart. He seemed determined to engage her in conversation, making no move to leave.

"I heard through the grapevine that you'd moved back to your hometown."

She nodded. No big surprise that he knew her current location, since the crew at the ski resort were like family. A couple of her ski friends had messaged her, wanting to know her whereabouts. But none of them had suggested they were planning an impromptu visit to Snowgum Creek.

She shuffled from one foot to the other. "Look, I need to get going."

He stood his ground. "Do you have lunch plans?"

Her mouth gaped open. No way would she willingly spend any more time in his company, let alone lunch. "Actually, yes."

He puffed out his chest, raising his chin. "Why don't you have lunch with me instead, show me the sights?"

She drew in a deep breath. "No, I have other plans."

Just then Luke's Jeep honked and the locks clicked. She glanced back at the clinic, a flicker of hope rising inside her.

Luke strode along the path, his head turned in her direction. He rushed straight past his Jeep, the brake lights flashing to indicate he had relocked it as he reached the sidewalk.

She let out an enormous sigh. Her rescuer had arrived.

Jason shoved his sunglasses up on his forehead, his eyes piercing. "Who is that guy?"

She attempted to smile, her confidence starting to return. "A friend and colleague."

Luke moved to her side, his mouth drawn into a frown. "Megan, are you ready to go?"

"Yes." She stood taller and stared at Jason. Time to move him on. "Enjoy your weekend in Snowgum Creek."

Jason nodded, his challenging gaze zeroing in on Luke before switching his attention back to her. "Megan, why don't we go out to dinner tonight, since you already have lunch plans? The Chinese restaurant looks good."

Chapter 6

Luke clenched his fists, ready to do battle with Megan's so-called friend. He sized up his opponent. His accent had a refined city twang, and his clothes screamed urban chic. No doubt he was the guy Megan wanted to avoid.

Megan's eyes widened. "No, Jason, I'm not going to have dinner with you."

Jason's smile faded. "Do you have plans tonight?"

"I'm really busy all weekend." She nibbled her lower lip. "I'm sure you can find your way around."

Luke took a step toward Jason, adrenaline pulsing through his muscles. "Snowgum Creek isn't a big town. The visitor center is near the post office, and they'll have information on what's happening in town."

Jason crossed his arms over his chest, his gaze focused on Megan. "I was hoping to see you this weekend."

She stared at the ground. "That's the way it goes. I'm working three jobs, and I'm really busy."

Luke lightly cupped Megan's elbow, leaning closer to her. "We need to go."

"Right. Bye." Megan spun on her heel and walked back toward the clinic.

Jason stood still, his jaw slack.

Luke pinned him with a long stare before following Megan.

She waited for him at his Jeep, her brows furrowed.

"What's going on?" he asked.

"He's the guy."

"I know, so why were you hanging around talking to him?"

"I wasn't." She placed her hands on her hips. "He wouldn't go away."

"Really? It didn't look like that to me."

She pursed her lips. "I tried to give him the hint that I wasn't interested in spending time with him."

"You didn't do a very good job."

"Well, I didn't want to be rude."

"Why?" He shook his head. "You don't think maybe he was the one who was out of line, bugging you to hang out with him?"

She let out an exasperated breath. "He's gone now, and I don't think I'll be seeing him again."

"I hope you're right. Now, are you ready for lunch?"

She nodded. "I was going to go home first, but we can go straight to the café instead, if that's easier."

"Sure, I'll drive you." He unlocked the Jeep and she made herself comfortable in the passenger seat. They drove a few streets into the center of town to a café not far from the church. Luke found a parking space outside the café.

They walked inside and Megan chose a table for two next to a window overlooking the street. She slid her coat over the back of her wooden seat, and perused the brightly colored menu.

He ignored the menu, planning to order his usual steak-and-vegetable pie with a side of fries. The café was known for its vegetarian options, sourcing its produce from local farmers whenever possible. It was a popular eatery, especially among the health-conscious Snowgum Creek residents.

He scanned the main street, questioning the wisdom of sitting beside a window. Jason had seemed determined to spend time with Megan. He couldn't discern whether Jason was just infatuated with Megan, which he could totally understand, or if he had more sinister intentions.

He met her gaze and relaxed, a slow smile curving up his lips. "What do you feel like?"

"Lentil soup and a side salad, I think. Something light but filling."

"A good choice. I'm having the meat pie. Would you like coffee?"

She nodded. "Latte, please."

"I'll be back in a minute." He headed over to the counter, joining the queue of people waiting to place their orders.

Sunlight filtered through the window, casting a golden glow over Megan. Her head was tipped forward as she typed something into her phone, a hint of a smile on her full lips.

Minutes later he placed their order and returned to their table.

Megan stashed her phone in her purse. "Is there anything in particular you want to talk about?"

"How's everything working out at the clinic?"

"Not bad. My personal training business is starting slow, but I'm getting there and making enough to cover my expenses."

"That's good to hear." He liked her determination to succeed despite the obstacles in her path. The old Megan would have quit by now, and run away to start a new adventure.

Her shoulders slumped. "It's not easy, and I know it takes time to build a following and a client base."

He nodded. "You'll get there if you persevere and don't give up."

"Maybe." She pressed her lips together, a vulnerable

look clouding her eyes. "A few people have mentioned they're not sure if I'll hang around."

No big surprise. He'd wondered the same thing himself more than once. "Do many people employ a trainer long-term?"

"They do in Sydney, but I assume most clients here would be short-term because I'm expensive."

"It's a luxury many can't afford." The farmers were having it tough. Even though the town was prosperous, no one was making megabucks compared to the incomes in the cities.

A waiter arrived with their lunch, and he tucked into the hearty meat pie.

Megan gulped in a sharp breath, her eyes wide. "Oh, no!"

He paused, his fork midair. "What's wrong?"

"He just walked in."

His stomach sank. "I told you that you were too nice to him. He probably followed us."

"Or he got lucky and saw your Jeep out front."

He resisted the urge to turn around. It was better to play it cool, and not let Jason know that his presence had disturbed Megan. "What's he doing?"

"Standing in the line to order something, and there's only one person waiting in front of him."

"He might be ordering something to go."

She shook her head. "He hates vegetarian food, and avoids eating wholesome foods. This style of café isn't his thing. I can't see him ordering something."

He rubbed his hand over the back of his neck, massaging a tension knot with his fingertips. "What do you want to do?"

"I don't know. I guess I can wait and see if he leaves or sits at a table. At least the ones closest to us are occupied."

"Something to be thankful for." He popped a few fries into his mouth, knowing it was likely they'd be leaving sooner rather than later.

She lowered her gaze, intent on eating her soup. "He just waved to me, and I ignored him."

Great. The guy wasn't taking no for an answer. The tables in the café were spaced out and the radio played in the background at a low volume. Thankfully the patrons at the nearby tables wouldn't be able to hear their quiet conversation.

He sipped his latte. "What's he doing now?"

She snuck a glance before concentrating on her salad. "He's sitting at a table across the room in my direct line of vision."

This whole situation was ridiculous. "You have to do something, otherwise he'll follow you around town all weekend."

She sighed. "Tell me about it. But I really don't think he'd listen if I told him to go away."

"You're probably right, but he could get desperate and do something unexpected."

"What can I do? I can't report him to the police just because I think he's annoying. They'd laugh me out of the station."

"Do you feel threatened?"

"It bothers me that he's here, more so than when I used to see him all the time at the ski fields."

"I understand. It took effort and planning for him to come here this weekend. Does he know where you live?"

She shook her head. "I haven't given my address to anyone he knows, and my car is parked in my garage. He may assume I'm living at the farm, but he'd have trouble finding it without the address and specific directions."

He held her shaky gaze, his tone serious. "I'm concerned about your safety tonight, especially since you live alone."

"I was going to hang out at home, catch up on chores and maybe watch a movie."

"Is he still watching you?"

She nodded. "I think his gaze has remained fixed on me the entire time."

"That's not a good sign. I'm on call after nine, but I have an idea that should work."

"What is it?"

"Would you like to come out to dinner with me tonight at the Chinese restaurant?"

She narrowed her eyes. "Why? I mean, what do you think that would achieve?"

"A lot. Let him think that we're together, and he doesn't have a chance with you. If we have dinner tonight as well as lunch, he should naturally draw that conclusion."

She leaned forward on her elbows, cradling her chin. "I don't need you to rescue me."

"Really?"

"I can handle the situation, somehow."

He shook his head. "You attempted to get rid of him by telling him to enjoy his weekend. I'd hardly call that taking care of the situation."

"So, what do you get out of this dinner deal?"

He gave her a charming smile. "A companion who will be happy to eat early, and won't be cranky when I bail on her at nine." It gave him an opportunity to ensure she was safe, and drive her to her parents' farm if Jason continued to stalk her.

She picked at her salad, spearing a slice of cucumber with her fork. "Do you think dinner will work?"

He nodded. "It could be fun, although we may need to act like we're together."

She tipped her head to the side. "What exactly are you suggesting?"

"Only that you drop the hostile stare and look as if you like spending time with me."

She let out a big sigh. "Okay, you win. What time should I be ready?"

"I'll make a booking for six."

"I guess I should wear something nice so it looks like we're on a real date."

He nodded. "Appearances count for everything tonight." He intended to make sure Jason knew he stood no chance of gaining Megan's affections. If only Luke's heart would cooperate with his plan, and realize he was only doing this to help her out of a sticky situation.

Megan's doorbell pealed at ten minutes to six. "Luke, I'm coming." She fastened the strap on her heel and made her way to the front door.

Luke stood on the other side of her screen door, looking effortlessly handsome in a full-length winter coat.

She smiled. "Hey, you're right on time."

He frowned. "Why did you call out to me?"

She raised her hands in the air, perplexed by his terse tone. "Because I knew it was you."

"How did you know? Did you install a camera out here?"

She bit back a sharp retort. "I heard your Jeep on the drive, and it was obviously you because I was expecting you right now."

He shook his head. "I could have been Jason, and your voice would have let him know he'd found the right house."

"I seriously doubt I'll see him tonight." She slipped her arms into her warm woolen coat, stepped outside and closed her front door. "He didn't approach me or follow us out of the café at lunch. His appearance at the café could have been a coincidence."

He ran his fingers through his short hair. "Your determination to see the best in people is going to get you into trouble."

"Maybe, but aren't people innocent until proven guilty?"

"When it concerns your safety, they're guilty until proven innocent. You need to take this situation more seriously."

She shrugged. "I think you're overreacting."

"A good friend of mine was stalked a couple of years ago, and it didn't end well."

She sucked in a sharp breath. "Is she okay?"

"She is now, but she went through a really rough time for a while."

"I'm sorry to hear that."

"The thing is, she didn't realize how serious the situation was until it was too late."

She walked beside him to his Jeep. "That's scary."

"Jason may be harmless, but I care about you and want to make sure you're safe."

Her heart skipped a beat, warmth filling her at the knowledge that he still cared for her. She felt safe and protected when she was with him, an alien feeling after living a carefree life with only a few significant emotional attachments.

He opened her car door. "You're looking very stylish tonight."

"Thank you." She grinned. "I'm glad I pass muster."

A wide smile brought an appreciative sparkle to his eyes. "Oh, you most definitely pass."

A blush rose up her cheeks. She turned her head away as she stepped up into her seat, hoping he missed her reaction to his compliment.

They drove past the restaurant and Luke found a parking spot across the street. Snowgum Creek buzzed with activity tonight. A number of people, including young families, wandered along the sidewalk. Tourists often stopped overnight at the hotels in town on their way to the ski fields.

Luke cupped her elbow and guided her toward the Chinese restaurant. Heads turned as they walked together, and a number of admiring female glances were sent in Luke's direction.

She let out a deep breath, feeling as though she was on a real date with Luke. They used to dine at the Chinese restaurant years ago, a favorite haunt because Luke loved Chinese food.

They approached the entrance to the restaurant. He held the door open, a perfect gentleman as he allowed her to step inside first.

She gave him a bright smile as they waited in the foyer. "You do realize the whole town may draw the wrong conclusion and assume we are dating for real?"

He reached for her hand, holding it briefly, his gaze warm. "I don't care. Your safety is more important than harmless gossip."

She nodded, enjoying the moment. She couldn't remember the last time she'd felt this comfortable on a dinner date, even if it was a pretense. The men she had dated over the years often had expectations she wasn't prepared to fulfill.

A waiter led them to a table in a secluded corner. It offered privacy and a good view of the entire restaurant, including the reception desk.

Luke chose the seat backing onto the wall and looking

out over the restaurant. "This time he can spend the evening staring at your back."

She settled into her seat, the skirt of her long flowing dress swirling over her legs. "Sounds like a good plan."

He picked up the menu. "What do you feel like?"

"I'll have what you're having."

He raised an eyebrow. "How do you know what I'll order?"

"Beef with black beans, and sweet and sour pork. Are they still your favorites?"

"You have a good memory."

"We ate those dishes many times in this restaurant." Happy memories flittered through her mind, bringing a big smile to her lips. "Or have you changed your preferences?"

He chuckled. "I do like satay chicken, and I'm not as fond of the black beans. I now prefer cashew nuts with my beef."

"I like all of those options, so you can choose what we eat."

"You're easy to please. I remember you being fussy about food."

"Not anymore. I have built some flexibility into my diet."

He nodded and placed their order with a hovering waiter. Before long the steaming dishes were delivered to their table.

She inhaled the concoction of scents, blending together to arouse her appetite.

"What would you like first?"

"Definitely the satay chicken and fried rice."

He served a portion of each on their plates. "May I say grace?"

"Sure." She closed her eyes, not used to praying in

public. Years ago she wouldn't have thought twice about saying the blessing in a restaurant.

"Lord, thank You for this good food and good company. Amen."

"Amen." She opened her eyes, meeting his intense gaze. "Thanks for inviting me to dinner tonight."

"You're welcome. Let's dig in."

She sampled the chicken, and suppressed a sigh. It melted on her tongue, the spicy flavors exploding in her mouth. "This is good."

"Yep. They still do the best Chinese in the district."

They chatted as they ate, and she remembered why she had liked dating him. He was an entertaining dinner companion, and there were no awkward lulls in their conversation.

He leaned back in his seat, the plates of food on their table nearly empty. "Can I tempt you with fried ice cream?"

She shook her head. "I'm full, and I couldn't eat another thing."

"How about jasmine tea?"

"I never say no to tea."

He signaled a waiter and ordered a pot of tea for two.

She grinned. "It seems like you didn't need to take me out to dinner after all."

"And miss the pleasure of your company?"

"Jason hasn't found us, so your fears are unfounded."

He drew his brows together. "You just spoke too soon."

Her throat constricted and she swallowed hard. "He's here."

"At the front of the line at the reception desk, staring right at us."

"He might be ordering something to go."

"We'll see. I think we should leave after we enjoy our tea."

"I agree there's no point letting his presence ruin our evening."

The waiter appeared with a teapot and two miniature cups. Luke requested the bill, tension radiating on his face.

She opened her purse.

"No, this is my treat."

"Are you sure?"

He nodded. "I always pay when I ask a lady to dinner."

"Thank you." She poured their tea, inhaling the relaxing aroma of jasmine.

The waiter returned and Luke perused the bill, placing cash inside the leather-bound folder.

She sipped her tea, the reality of Jason's presence weighing on her mind. No way would she turn around and see if he was still in the restaurant. The last thing she wanted to do was encourage his attention.

Luke rested his arms on the table. "You've gone quiet on me."

"I'm thinking."

"He's still standing in the reception area, and I assume he's ordered something to go."

She sipped the remains of her tea. "I'm ready to leave if you are."

He stood. "Let's go."

She walked beside Luke toward the door, and he threaded his fingers through hers. The familiar gesture brought a smile to her lips and lightened her mood.

Jason leaned against a wall, his eyes widening at their approach. "Hey, Megan."

She ignored him, staying close beside Luke, reassured by his presence.

Luke leaned closer to her ear, his voice low. "Keep walking and don't look back."

She pushed the outside door open, the urge to flee building in her mind.

"Megan, wait," Jason said.

She looked up at Luke. "He's following us."

Chapter 7

Luke tightened his grip on Megan's hand, pulling her to a halt under a streetlight. "I'm going to deal with this now."

Megan gasped. "Please don't get into a fight."

"I won't." He tipped her chin up with his thumb, looking deep into her eyes. "But I need you to follow my lead, okay?"

She nodded and took a step back, half standing behind him.

Jason sauntered toward them, an arrogant tilt to his head as his calculating gaze swept over them.

Luke stood his ground. "What do you want?"

"I just want to talk to Megan."

"She doesn't want to talk to you."

He smirked. "She can't speak for herself?"

Megan took a big step forward, her arms crossed over her torso. "I'm busy and you're interrupting our evening."

"Yes." Luke draped his arm over Megan's shoulders, pulling her closer to his side. "Did Megan tell you that we dated for four years?"

Jason shook his head, a puzzled expression shadowing his face. "Are you two together?"

Megan's arm tensed around his waist, her breathing shallow. "It's none of your business what I do in my personal life."

Jason raised his hands, palms facing up. "All right, I get it. I thought you liked me but you've obviously changed your mind."

Megan turned toward Luke, warmth radiating from her blue eyes. "Luke is very important to me."

His pulse raced, her heartfelt words soothing old wounds.

Jason flinched, his face pale. "Okay, I won't bother you again." He walked back toward the restaurant, shoulders slumped.

Luke stepped back, his attention focused on Megan. "Are you okay?"

She nodded, her eyes moist. "Thank you."

"You're welcome. It's good he left of his own accord, without me having to force the issue." His fist had been clenched, ready to take on Jason if he'd pushed harder to see Megan.

She shuddered. "I'm glad he got the message."

He walked with her to his Jeep and opened her door.

Lips pressed together, she stepped up into the vehicle and settled in her seat.

He fastened his seat belt and switched on the ignition. "Are you sure you're okay?"

She covered her face with her hands, her head bent forward. "I'm such an idiot."

He reversed out of the parking space, aware of the scrutiny they were receiving from a number of passersby. "No, you're not. You weren't to know how things would pan out."

"I didn't realize that he thought I was interested in him." She sat up straight, flicking her hair out of her eyes. "I told him a few years ago, when he asked me out, that I wasn't interested in a relationship with him."

"Maybe he thought you'd changed your mind."

"I've no idea why he would think that."

He stayed silent, unwilling to initiate a conversation about her inability to deal with conflict. This time the problem she'd run from had caught up with her.

He turned onto a road leading out of town. "We're going to take the scenic route back to your house, just to make sure we're rid of him."

"A good idea." She swung around in her seat, the full moon lighting the interior of the Jeep. "I'm sorry you got caught up in this mess."

"It's no big deal, and you know where to find me if you need to be rescued again."

"Ouch." Her tone lightened. "I'm not a helpless female who can't take care of herself."

"I never thought that for a minute."

"What were you thinking?"

He tapped his fingers on the steering wheel. "That you need new friends. Are all your friends at the ski resort like him?"

"No, the rest of them are kind of normal. I miss hanging out with them."

"Are you going back next year?"

"I haven't thought that far ahead."

He nodded. At least she was honest. He had the next few years of his life in Snowgum Creek mapped out. His new house was coming along, the frame now up. The house should be ready for him to move in later this year, assuming there were no more delays.

The high-beam headlights illuminated the country road and he turned onto another road, taking a different route back into town. They should arrive at her cottage within ten minutes.

She smiled, stretching out her arms and legs. "This seat is comfy."

"I'm glad you approve."

"Thanks again for tonight. It was fun to hang out, like old times."

"We should try to catch up more often." Despite the drama at the end of dinner, he'd enjoyed her company. She was fun to be around, and he'd missed her easy companionship.

Her face relaxed in the moonlight. "We need to schedule a cycling trip up in the mountains."

"A Sunday ride would work for me."

"What about church?"

"We could go to the night service. Why don't we organize a full day trip, and stop somewhere nice for lunch?"

"Are you offering to make lunch?"

"I'm not completely useless in the kitchen, and I can make sandwiches."

She laughed. "I'm happy to know you won't starve. We can compare schedules tomorrow at church, and choose a date."

"Okay. Are you going to the morning service?"

"Yes." She paused. "The last place Jason would expect to find me is church."

"Really?"

"I visited a couple of churches years ago when I first started working at the ski resort, but I didn't find a congregation where I fit in."

"What didn't you like about them?"

"To be honest, it seemed like everyone who was single and in my age group was looking for a spouse." She shook her head. "That wasn't one of my goals, and I found it hard to relate to them."

"That makes sense."

"My work friends didn't go to church." She sighed. "This probably sounds terrible, but I felt like a second-class citizen because I was single and had no aspirations to get married in my twenties."

"You're not the first person to have this conversation with me." His friend Emily had experienced similar issues in previous churches. "Do you feel like that at Snowgum Creek Community Church?"

"No, but it's my childhood church and I grew up with half the congregation. I feel at home there."

"I'm glad." He'd been praying that she'd use her time in Snowgum Creek to remember and explore the vibrant faith from her youth.

Lord, thank You for bringing Megan back to our church family, and I pray she will continue to feel welcome and grow in her faith.

Megan sat beside Kate in a padded outdoor chair on the back deck of Jack and Kate's home. Her brother had invited Luke's family over for a barbecue lunch after church. They were all playing cricket on the lawn, and laughing as Ben's dog, Lily, chased the ball around the yard.

Luke held the wooden cricket bat, and Rachel stood in the wicketkeeper position behind a plastic trash bin they were using as a wicket. Ben and Jack were taking turns bowling, while Amy and the children fielded in various positions around the yard.

Megan smiled, her gaze focused on Luke. He wore a fitted sweater and jeans, accentuating his lean cyclist's build. She'd seen a lot of Luke since the incident with Jason over a month ago. She'd even had pizza with Kara at his and Rachel's home after church one evening. To her surprise, she found she now liked Kara and enjoyed hanging out with her.

Kate rubbed her stomach. "I think I ate too much for lunch."

"Oh, no, are you feeling okay?"

"I'm starting to get heartburn after I eat."

Megan wrinkled her nose. "Not fun."

Luke's nephew, Declan, bowled a good overarm delivery, and Luke hit the ball high into the air. His niece, Chloe, ran for the ball. She caught it clean in the outfield before Lily could reach it.

Megan clapped, impressed by Chloe's coordination. "Great catch."

"I reckon Luke hit that one to Chloe on purpose."

"Of course. According to Amy, he dotes on the kids."

Kate smiled. "He'll make a great dad one day."

Megan lowered her gaze, her neck warm under her scarf and jacket. Kate had echoed her thoughts as she watched Luke play with the kids.

"Speaking of Luke, he's heading our way."

Megan's heart lightened as he waved and sent her a broad smile. She'd told Jason the truth when she'd said Luke was an important person in her life.

He leaped up the steps and dropped into the chair beside Megan. "What are you two up to?"

Megan smiled. "Watching your family play cricket."

He winked. "I would have tried harder if I'd known you were paying attention."

"No way." She laughed. "You're too busy indulging your niece by hitting shots she can catch."

"You really were watching." He grinned and turned to Kate. "How are you feeling?"

Kate wriggled in her seat. "Pretty good. I can feel the baby moving."

"Really?" Megan dragged her chair closer to Kate. "Can you feel bub now?"

Kate nodded. "I used to only feel flutters but now I think I'm feeling the baby kick."

"That's normal for this stage of your pregnancy," Luke said. "Your next prenatal appointment with me must be coming up soon."

"Yes, next week. I'm due to have another scan and see my obstetrician in Sunny Ridge next month."

Kate had booked a birthing suite in the maternity ward at Sunny Ridge Hospital. Megan couldn't wait to finally meet her little nephew or niece.

Kate placed her hand on her belly. "The baby is on the move."

"Can I feel it?" she asked.

"I think so." Kate smiled and positioned Megan's hand on her abdomen.

Megan kept her hand still on Kate's rounded stomach. A slight pulsing motion fluttered under her palm. "I can feel something."

Luke met her gaze, warmth filling his golden eyes. "If you're patient, the baby might change position for you."

She held her breath, waiting. A sharp movement jostled her hand and her heart melted. "Wow, there really is a baby in there!"

Megan's face lit up, and Luke's pulse accelerated as he drank in the awe and wonder shining in her animated eyes. He'd never seen her exhibit any maternal instincts until the moment when she felt the baby kick inside Kate's abdomen.

Kate smiled. "It explains the heartburn."

"It's amazing." Megan grinned, her hand still resting on Kate's abdomen. "I want to feel another kick."

Luke laughed. "You'll have plenty of opportunity over the next few months. The kicks and punches will only get stronger."

Megan dropped her hand. "I'm so glad I'll be living close by when the baby arrives."

Kate shifted in her seat, straightening her back. "You'll make a wonderful aunt."

"You think so?" she asked.

Luke nodded. "You'll be the fun aunty Megan."

Kate chuckled. "And you'll get to play with the baby while I'm in a sleep-deprived haze and doing all the hard work."

Megan let out a contented sigh. "I'm going to enjoy spending time with the baby."

"I'm sure you will." Was Megan serious about wanting to play a significant role in her niece or nephew's life? He was drawn to Megan, and wanted to spend more time with her.

He couldn't help wondering what direction their lives would have taken if she'd accepted his marriage proposal. Could she commit to living in Snowgum Creek long-term? Did he dare entertain the idea that their relationship could evolve into something more serious?

A week later, Megan tapped on Bruce's office door in the administration building at Sunny Ridge Hospital. The sports medicine doctor had summoned her for an impromptu meeting, and a queasy feeling filled her stomach. Had she done something wrong?

"Megan, come in and take a seat." Bruce sat behind his desk, his glasses on the tip of his nose as he typed something into his computer.

She sat on the other side his desk, her hands clasped tightly in her lap. In half an hour she was meeting Luke's friend Emily in the hospital cafeteria for lunch. She'd met Emily at Snowgum Creek Community Church a couple of weeks ago, and they were fast becoming good friends.

Bruce looked up, smiling. "Thanks for coming at short notice. I've been meaning to talk to you for a while, but my schedule has been full."

She nodded. "I understand." All the doctors in the hospital, Emily included, seemed to be overworked with a large patient caseload.

"So, how are you finding your work here and at Snowgum Creek? Are you enjoying your hospital role?"

She nodded, unsure of the reason behind his questions. "It's going well, and I like working with the patients."

"That's good. I've heard a number of glowing reports about your work. You're doing a great job."

"Thank you." She smiled, her body relaxing. "I appreciate the feedback and I feel like I've settled in well."

"The bean counters haven't made a decision about your position when the twelve-month contract ends."

"I'm not expecting to have a definite answer for at least another six months."

He nodded, his gaze thoughtful. "I doubt you'll hear any earlier, because the future of your position will depend on the outcome of the next government funding allocation."

"That's okay. I'm happy with the twelve-month contract, and I don't need to make any decisions until next year."

"Actually, that's why I wanted to talk to you. I'm impressed with your work and wanted to chat about potential career opportunities."

She lifted a brow. "What exactly do you mean? There's really nowhere else to go within the hospital system."

He leaned forward in his seat, his hands clasped together on his desk. "Have you thought about doing a master's degree program?"

"Yes and no." She smoothed her skirt over her knee. "I tend to travel a lot and I usually work at the ski fields in winter."

"Which is why I think you could be the perfect master's degree candidate for my new research project."

She sat straighter, his words capturing her full attention. "What do you have in mind?"

His smile broadened. "In July next year I'm starting a research project on skiing injuries. The two-year project will be based in Sydney, but we'll be spending some time during winter doing research in the Snowy Mountains."

"Wow, I don't know what to say. It sounds like an incredible opportunity."

"It will be intense, and a lot of hard work, but it would combine your two interests in sports science and skiing."

She nodded. "I like that idea."

"My understanding is your current contract ends in May, giving you time to relocate to Sydney. I believe your practical knowledge and love of skiing would be an asset to the project."

Her stomach lurched, her hopes of taking on the research position and living for part of the year in Snowgum Creek evaporating. "When do you need an answer?"

"Within the next six or seven weeks. You'll need to apply for the master's degree program this year, although I can't imagine you'll have any difficulties securing a place. It's easier when you're part of a funded research project."

She nodded. "Thanks for offering me this opportunity. I'll think about it and get back to you."

"Sure." He ran his fingers through his wavy hair, highlighted with blond tips. "Unfortunately I'll need a decision from you before you'll hear if your current contract can be extended. But, since you move around a lot, you'll probably be ready for a new challenge next year."

"Okay." Her mind spun with numerous possibilities for next year. She'd never dreamed she'd be offered the opportunity to combine her love of skiing with a master's research program. It seemed like her ultimate dream job, but it would mean leaving Snowgum Creek. And leaving Luke, again.

She walked out of Bruce's office in a daze. What would Luke say if he knew about this opportunity? Her heart was torn between staying in Snowgum Creek with her family and Luke, and chasing her career ambitions.

Over the past few weeks she'd become closer to Luke, and her feelings for him were growing stronger the more time they spent together. He'd established his life and career in Snowgum Creek. If she accepted the research position, she'd destroy any chance of a future with Luke.

Chapter 8

Two weeks later, Megan walked up the front path to the clinic. Emily's car was parked on the drive beside Luke's Jeep. Luke was heading out of town tonight for a weekend camp with the church youth group, and Emily was his replacement at the clinic and hospital.

Megan entered the reception area. "Hey, Emily."

Emily smiled. "Megan, I'm so glad to see you."

She gave Emily a brief hug, happy to see her new friend in Snowgum Creek. "I'm so looking forward to hanging out with you this weekend."

"Let's hope the hospital is quiet tomorrow night, otherwise I'll be sleeping all day Sunday."

"Have you got time for coffee?"

"Sure do. I'm free for the rest of the day." She followed Megan to the staff room. "What about you?"

"I have one client in half an hour, then a quiet afternoon until I start my personal training sessions at the gym at five."

"Business is still slow?"

"Yep." She collected two mugs and started making their lattes, her back facing the entrance to the room. "Is Luke around?"

"He's with a patient." Emily placed Luke's keys on the counter beside the coffee machine. "I've just left my gear in the spare room at his house."

"Since we have his keys, we could always take Luke's Jeep for a spin. It doesn't look like he's taken it off-road very often."

"Oh, really?" Luke's deep voice resonated through the room. "And where exactly are you planning to take my Jeep?"

Emily giggled. "I think you're sprung."

She grabbed Luke's clean coffee mug off the drainer and spun around, catching his gaze. "Somewhere in the mountains. We could head northeast on the old road to Canberra."

"A good plan, except I need to leave in three hours to drive Kara and a couple of the kids to the camp." His eyes twinkled. "We could go for a drive together up in the mountains sometime."

"You don't trust me with your Jeep?"

"You have a habit of getting bogged."

Megan pouted. "That wasn't my fault. Jack told us to go ahead and gave us the wrong directions."

Emily lifted a manicured brow. "I'd like to hear that story sometime."

Megan handed a latte to Emily. "It's not very interesting. We got stuck in the mountains with no phone reception, and had to wait for Jack to return with my father to tow us out of the mud."

Luke stood beside her and pocketed his keys, his gaze intense. "We found creative ways to fill the time."

Megan turned away from Luke and Emily, warmth flooding her face as old memories resurfaced. She stared at the coffee machine, continuing to make their lattes. How could he still have the power to make her blush like a teenager?

Emily dragged a chair out from under the table. "So, Luke, what are your plans for the camp?"

"I don't have all the details of our itinerary, but I do know we'll be home in time for church on Sunday night."

"Megan and I will plan to be there."

"Sounds good." Her face cooler, Megan passed a coffee mug to Luke. His fingertips skimmed the back of her hand, and a jolt of awareness flowed through her.

His magnetic gaze held her captive. "Thanks for the latte."

"You're welcome." She drew in a steadying breath before picking up her mug and sitting beside him at the table.

He stirred sugar into his coffee. "Now, you girls better not have too much fun without me."

Emily flicked her streaked blond hair back over her shoulders. "We'll behave ourselves, and we can catch up with you after church on Sunday night if I'm not too tired."

He raised an eyebrow. "You're worried about being tired? You won't be spending two nights in a cabin supervising a bunch of kids who won't want to sleep."

Megan grinned. "And stopping them from sneaking out during the night."

Emily sipped her coffee. "Now the truth is coming out. Is that what you two used to do at camp?"

She raised her hands. "Don't look at me. It was usually Luke's grand plan to sneak out of our rooms."

"Really?" Emily switched her attention to Luke. "You haven't told me these stories, and how many years have we known each other?"

He shrugged. "The kids at camp won't get away with anything because I know all the tricks."

Megan stirred the froth into her latte. "He's the one who led me astray with his harebrained ideas."

"As if Emily will believe you were completely innocent." He relaxed in his chair, cradling his coffee mug.

"Would you like to tell her who got the bright idea to go swimming in a creek at midnight?"

She giggled. "We were at a summer camp and it was a stinking-hot night. Everything went to plan until we spotted a snake. Amy's scream woke up everyone within a ten-mile radius, including all the leaders."

Emily shook her head. "I'm glad I was never your youth group leader."

Luke chuckled. "We weren't too bad compared to some of the antics I've seen as a leader."

Megan nodded. "We had lots of fun together."

"I can see that." Emily's blue eyes held a speculative gleam. "How long did you two date?"

"Four years and three months," Luke said.

Megan shot him a surprised look. "You remember the exact dates."

He stood. "I'm good at math, and my next patient is due any minute. I should be finished for the day within the next hour."

"No problem," Emily said. "We're meeting Rachel at your place around three-thirty."

"Okay, I'll see you there." He strolled out of the room, his step light.

Megan drank her coffee, distracted by Luke's comment. He had proposed four years and three months to the day after they'd started dating. His references to their previous relationship had stirred up feelings that had lain dormant for a long time. It was going to feel like a long weekend without him around.

Luke yawned and shuffled into the dining room at the campsite for breakfast. One night down, and he was already fatigued. How was he going to survive another night with very little sleep? This was worse than being on call.

Hopefully their long Saturday-afternoon hike after lunch would help all the kids sleep well tonight.

Kara joined him at the end of the queue for breakfast. "You look shattered."

"It was a very long night."

"Tell me about it. The girls wouldn't shut up until after three."

"Why do we do this to ourselves?"

She chuckled. "Because someone did it for us."

He nodded, his thoughts returning to Megan. She'd plagued his mind last night, memories from their youth flooding back as he had lain awake on the hard bunk-bed mattress. She hadn't said much about the camp or his youth group activities, and he struggled to get a gauge on her faith.

He was pleased Megan and Emily had hit it off. They had a lot in common, and Emily would be a helpful person for Megan to talk to about faith matters.

The kids had congregated at the tables, wide-awake and looking as if they'd all had a brilliant night's sleep. He collected a plate of bacon, hash browns and scrambled eggs, and followed Kara to the one empty table in the corner.

Luke's mother had hoped he'd marry either Kara or Emily. He'd been friends with Kara since they were kids, and she was more like a sister than a friend. He'd become best friends with Emily at med school, meeting her at a Christian group on campus right after Megan had left him. Emily looked like a model, but there was never going to be anything romantic happening between them.

A certain brunette had once again pushed herself to the forefront of his mind. Despite his growing attraction to Megan, he was reluctant to invest more time in a relationship that could potentially go nowhere. She was still secretive and evasive. He had a strong sense she wasn't telling him the full story about her plans for next year.

Kara poured him a cup of coffee. "You look like you need this."

"Thanks." Somehow he'd managed to set up his life so he had no time to rest. He savored this break away, a chance to reflect and focus on the important things in life.

Kara tasted her coffee, wrinkling her nose. "Ugh, this instant coffee is really bad."

"Did you bring coffee?"

She shook her head. "I packed in a mad rush yesterday."

"Me, too. Emily arrived at my place yesterday, and I was trying to pack while she and Megan were visiting with Rachel." His sister sat at a table on the other side of the room, surrounded by a group of teen girls.

Kara tilted her head to the side, her gaze thoughtful. "I noticed you've been spending a fair bit of time with Megan."

He nodded. No doubt Kara had heard the gossip that had circulated around town after he'd had dinner with Megan at the Chinese restaurant a few months ago.

"You need to be careful with Megan."

"I know."

She frowned. "I'm serious, Luke. She seems more settled now but do people really change?"

He narrowed his eyes. "That's a bit harsh."

"Is it?" Her voice softened. "I was there eight years ago, and I know how badly she hurt you. It's great that she's back in church, but I don't know if she's prepared to stay in Snowgum Creek."

Kara's words echoed Jack's thoughts. But what if Megan had matured and was prepared to settle down? Was he willing to take a risk, and deal with the fallout if she did leave town? Could he restructure his life to have more flexibility?

Lord, please give me wisdom regarding Megan, and help me to discern Your will for my life.

Megan typed up her notes for her last client at the clinic. Her Saturday morning had been busy, starting with a few personal training sessions at the gym before a full schedule of appointments at the clinic. She had lunch plans with Emily before they drove out to the farm midafternoon. Kate had bailed on their lunch date, only remembering this morning that Jack had made other plans.

She switched off her computer and packed up her desk. What was Luke doing now at the camp? The old routine was a talk or group Bible study in the morning before some kind of exhausting afternoon activity designed to tire out all the kids.

Megan had fond memories of hiking with Luke, trying to outdo him by reaching the end of the trail first. They'd always competed against each other, which had only intensified when they started dating. She'd enjoyed the challenge of battling wits with him, knowing he treated her as an equal and gave her only a few concessions.

She grabbed her purse and made her way to the staff room. The coffee machine awaited her, and she brewed a strong latte before sitting at the table. She opened her ebook reader and flicked over to her Bible file. The list of books in the Old and New Testaments displayed on the screen.

She chewed on her lower lip. Which book in the Bible should she start reading first? It had been ages since she'd felt the urge to open her Bible.

Emily walked into the staff room. "That coffee smells good."

"Yep. Are you finished for the morning?"

"Nearly." She picked up a mug and switched on the coffee machine. "I have a cancellation now, and about twenty minutes until my next patient arrives."

"Would you like me to make your coffee?"

She shook her head. "I'm good. I need to practice my barista skills, and I don't want to interrupt your reading."

"It's okay. I can't decide which book of the Bible to read."

Emily lifted a brow. "What are you looking for?"

"I don't know." She leaned back in her chair, staring at the ceiling. "I feel lost, with no idea of which direction to head."

"You could read one of the wisdom books."

"I was thinking about Ecclesiastes, and how there are different seasons in life."

"Not a bad place to start." Emily pulled up a chair at the table opposite her. "We could always read it together."

"Yeah, I'd like that." She admired Emily's strong faith and commitment to her beliefs. Megan still believed and had faith, but it was a diluted version compared to when she was younger. Emily challenged her to reconnect with God in a meaningful way.

Emily smiled. "Have you told Luke about the research job?"

She shook her head. "I nearly told him a few times, but it just wasn't the right moment."

"Have you made a decision about it?"

"Not yet." She sighed. "It's the opportunity of a lifetime as far as my career is concerned. But I've also invested time in setting up my business here. If the hospitals are prepared to renew the contract, I'm not sure if they'll find it easy to recruit someone who is willing to work part-time hours."

Emily nodded. "That's a good point."

"A three-day-a-week job in two different towns isn't going to attract that many applicants when they can earn better money in the city."

"True, but there's no guarantee they'll renew your contract."

"I know. My manager at the ski resort is keeping my job open for next year. Now the situation with Jason is sorted, I have no reason to not return to my old job." She frowned. "Unless I stay in Snowgum Creek or take the research job."

"What about Luke? How does he factor into your decision making?"

"That's the problem." She twisted a loose lock of hair around her finger. "He has set up his life here in Snowgum Creek, and I can't expect him to pack up and follow me somewhere else."

"And he's building his new house."

"So I've heard, but I haven't seen it."

"Really?" Emily drew her brows together. "He gave me a tour the last time I visited Snowgum Creek."

"That's not surprising, since you're one of his best friends."

Emily leaned forward, cradling her chin in her hands. "You need to tell him about the job offer. I'll keep my mouth shut, but I can tell there's something more than friends going on between the two of you."

"Is it that obvious?"

"Yes. Luke's a great guy and he deserves to know the full story. Then together you can negotiate a way forward."

"What you're saying makes sense, but I don't want to upset the apple cart for no good reason."

"In what way?"

"If I don't say anything, and turn down the research job, then it saves him a lot of unnecessary angst."

"But you're not being honest." Emily frowned. "Wouldn't you like to know about this if you were in his position?"

"Maybe, but it's a deal breaker as far as a relationship is concerned."

"It doesn't have to be."

"I'd be gone for two years, with a full schedule and no time for a long-distance relationship. I can't expect him to put his life on hold. Plus the job could open doors for research opportunities overseas."

Emily nodded. "Is that the life you want?"

"That's the thing. I don't know what I want, and I've never really thought about chasing an overseas sports science career."

"It's a big decision, and I'll be praying for you."

"Thanks." She needed all the prayers she could get. Which option should she pick?

Lord, I know I don't pray very often, but I really need some guidance now. I can't deny I have feelings for Luke, and I don't know which career opportunity is the right one to pursue.

Chapter 9

Luke walked along the corridor in the main ward of Snow-gum Creek Hospital, scrolling through the messages on his phone. He smiled. Megan was already in the cafeteria, waiting to meet him for lunch.

He rubbed a weary hand over his tired eyes. He'd slept for only seven hours last night after coming home from the youth camp late yesterday afternoon, and he needed an early night tonight. He'd stayed up late talking with Emily and Rachel, and was paying for it today.

He entered the small cafeteria. Megan sat by herself at a table for two in the corner. Sunlight streamed through the window next to her, bringing out the auburn high-lights in her hair.

She looked up and smiled, her blue eyes gleaming. "I'm glad you could make it."

"Me, too." He sat opposite her, his awareness of her intensifying as his knee skimmed hers under the table. The line between friends and something more was blur-ring, and he'd given up the struggle to keep her out of his thoughts.

"Do you have time to eat?"

He nodded. "I'm not due back at the clinic for at least an hour."

"Wow, you're actually taking a lunch break."

"Over the weekend I decided I needed to create more balance in my life."

"I can understand why. Your schedule is crazy."

"I'm hoping to change that soon. Have you eaten?"

She shook her head. "I think I'll have a salad. The menu here isn't particularly appetizing."

"Caesar salad and a latte?"

"Yes, please."

He stood. "I'll be back in a minute." He made his way to the counter, placing their order with a young girl at the cash register before returning to Megan.

She slipped her phone into her purse. "What are you having?"

"A sandwich and coffee. It beats a muesli bar on the run. They'll bring it over to us soon."

"How'd you manage to get table service?"

He grinned. "A perk of being a doctor."

"Why am I surprised? You can charm everyone."

"The truth is they feel sorry for us poor overworked doctors."

She rolled her eyes. "Whatever. Are you free for an early-morning ride on Wednesday?"

"I think so. Are you seeing Emily in Sunny Ridge tomorrow?"

"We have lunch plans. Why?"

"Rachel dropped by the clinic this morning with a T-shirt Emily left behind at our place."

"No worries. I'll swing by the clinic on my way to the gym after work. Are you working until six?"

"I'm not sure. Do you have the keys with you? I can leave the T-shirt on your desk."

"Sounds good. You should do the cycle class with me tonight if you can escape early."

"We'll see what happens. My afternoons are usually too long."

The young girl brought their order to their table.

He thanked her and unwrapped his sandwich. "Now, Megan, what time do you want to leave on Wednesday morning?"

"My first P.T. session at the gym is at eight, so it would need to be really early."

"Sure. I should have caught up on sleep by then."

"Was the camp exhausting? You looked wiped out last night."

"Yes, it was good fun and we went on a really long hike."

"In the mountains?"

He nodded. "You remember the uphill trail that takes at least four hours to walk?"

"Did you see any red wallabies by the creek?"

"Yes, they're still congregating in the usual spot."

She smiled. "It's a pretty walk, and I love the spectacular mountain views."

He raised an eyebrow. "You could always become a youth group leader and join us on the hike next year."

"I don't know what I'm doing next year."

"When will you learn if the hospitals are renewing your contract?"

"Not until next year. I have the option of going back to the snow next winter."

"Really? Is that what you want to do?"

She squirmed in her seat, lowering her lashes. "I have time to think and pray before I need to make any big decisions."

"Fair enough." He was glad to hear she was praying about these decisions. Did her prayers include contemplating a future with him?

* * *

On Wednesday morning, Megan cruised with Luke on the cycle track that followed Snowgum Creek to the edge of town. A couple of gray kangaroos grazed nearby, the dew on the grass glistening in the morning sunlight.

She lowered the gears on her bike as they approached the crest of a hill. "Which way do you want to go?"

He cycled beside her, his legs pedaling in sync with hers. "To the outskirts of town. I have something I want to show you."

"Really? What is it?"

He laughed. "You'll just have to wait and see. We'll be there in less than ten minutes."

She scrunched her nose, her curiosity piqued. The look-out was in the opposite direction of where they were heading.

He rode ahead and peeled off the main track onto a rough dirt path that led back toward the road.

She followed behind, pumping her legs as he picked up speed and raced ahead in a cloud of dust. They'd already completed forty minutes of interval training, and it was time for a recovery session combined with a short break.

He wove through a maze of tree-lined streets, not a car moving in sight. She rode single file behind him, her throat scratchy. She couldn't wait to stop and take a long drink of iced water.

Luke turned onto the street that eventually led to his house high up on the hill overlooking the township. Surrounded by five acres, it was prime real estate and he'd demolished the old cottage the previous owners had lived in.

She'd seen his house-building progress from a distance, but she hadn't ventured into this exclusive part of town in years. The street was lined with acreages, the blocks becoming larger the farther they rode.

Before long they reached the gate to his property. He stopped beside a large barrel-shaped metal letter box, checking to see if he had any mail.

She pulled up next to him. "So, this is your new place."

He nodded, flicking through his mail before stashing it in a bag attached to the back of his bike. "What do you think?"

"It's a lovely location."

"I've had my eye on this place for years and grabbed it as soon as the previous owners put it on the market."

The grounds at the front, including a long gravel drive, were well maintained. Lawn and native shrubs were planted around a number of established gum trees. "I hope you're investing in a riding mower."

He laughed. "That's the first thing Ben said, too. Come on, I'll show you the house."

She rode beside him up the drive, admiring the impressive view of the township below. Following his lead, she stashed her bike under a tree and headed toward the wide front veranda that wrapped around two sides of the house.

He juggled a set of keys in his hands. "We've finally reached the lockup stage, after a number of delays."

"When will the house be ready?"

"Who knows? I'm on various tradesmen's waiting lists. Last week I managed to get the fixtures in the kitchen and bathroom installed. That was a big achievement."

She nodded as she stepped inside on the concrete floor and looked around. Luke gave her a tour of the sprawling single-level house. The bathrooms were the closest to being finished, needing only to be tiled and painted. He led her through three separate living areas, and showed her the laundry, study and triple garage.

"Wow." She stood in the spacious galley-style kitchen, envious of the enormous amount of counter space he had compared to her cottage kitchen. "You didn't cut any corners."

He shook his head. "That's why it's taking so long, but it's worth doing it properly. I'm installing ducted heating and air-conditioning, plus a pool, spa and entertaining area out back."

Leaning back on the new granite counter, she held his warm gaze. "You're creating a beautiful home."

"That's the plan. I don't intend to move away from here for a very long time."

She swallowed hard, the implications of his words seeping into her mind. He had built this home with a family in mind. It would easily accommodate three or four children. She could see a couple of mischievous boys with golden eyes running around the house, playing outdoors in the trees and swimming in the pool.

She gulped down a couple of mouthfuls of water from her bottle, the cool liquid refreshing her parched throat. This could be her life, her future. The life she'd be living now if she'd accepted Luke's marriage proposal eight years ago.

He smiled. "Do you want to see the back of the property, or has time run away from us?"

She glanced at her watch. "I need to head back, but you can stay longer if you need to do some work here."

He shook his head. "I'm done and ready for a long sprint. It's downhill all the way home."

"That's a relief. Thanks for showing me your house."

"I'm glad you like it, and you didn't make any comments about the size of the kitchen like the rest of my family."

"What did they say?"

"That it's a waste that I'll have the largest and most functional kitchen out of everyone in the family."

She chuckled. "They have a point, but they could always volunteer to come over and cook for you."

"That's my comeback. One day I may even have the time to learn how to cook properly."

"You're living in a dream world if you think your current workload will drop anytime soon."

"Then I'll have to switch to plan B."

"Which is?"

His eyes twinkled. "Find someone who'll cook for me."

She lowered her lashes, the challenge in his voice stirring her heart. Did he view her as a potential wife, after everything that had happened? Could she be happy living here as Luke's wife, raising his children?

She turned away and picked up her bottle. "I need to get moving."

"Sure, I'll lock up behind you and meet you out front."

She rushed toward the front door, her pulse galloping. She'd spent her life running from responsibility and long-term commitments. Was she capable of settling down in one place, living in one house, without becoming restless for new adventures?

Megan sat next to Luke in the back row of the Snowgum Creek Community Church. The morning sun filtered through the stained-glass windows on the eastern side of the church. After embarking on two midweek outdoor cycling sessions with Luke this week, including her first visit to his future home, she'd hung out with Rachel and Kara last night at his house.

She snuck a sideways glance in his direction while half listening to the sermon. He was bleary-eyed, with dark shadows under his eyes highlighting his fatigue. He'd been in and out all evening, on call at the hospital. His life was chaotic, and she understood why he wanted to lighten his workload.

The sermon was the second part in a series on the book of James. Their pastor addressed the issue of faith being alive and demonstrated by Christian service. She leaned back in her seat, his words catching her attention. Her faith had become stagnant in recent years. She didn't have the depth in her personal relationship with God that she'd seen in her friends and Luke.

She closed her eyes, absorbing the pastor's words like a dry garden receiving rain for the first time after a long drought. She prayed that God would show her what she needed to do, what He wanted her to do.

Megan opened her eyes, a new clarity and sense of peace permeating her mind. This was why Luke had chosen to be a youth group leader and now sat beside her, exhausted. He valued doing God's work. But he'd taken on too many activities and suffered the consequences.

She had the opposite problem. Her life choices reflected her desire to please herself, with little regard for others or the need to do God's work in the world.

She let out a big sigh. Her deliberate refusal to address issues and deal with conflict had created massive problems in her life. What if she'd had the courage to speak up last year and tell Jason his actions made her uncomfortable? Would the conversation have deterred him from following her to Snowgum Creek? Or was his obsession with her inevitable, irrespective of how she handled the situation?

The service moved into a time of prayer and she bowed her head, reflecting on her life choices in recent years. Emily had given her wise advice and helped her work through a number of issues. She understood why Luke valued his friendship with Emily.

She'd let go of her long-held grudge against Kara, recognizing it was based on childish issues that no longer existed. Kara had made an effort to befriend her, and they were now spending a lot of time together with Luke and Rachel.

She stood for the last song. Luke swayed in her direction, his arm brushing against her as he regained his balance.

Megan leaned in closer, whispering in his ear, "Are you okay?"

"I'm just tired, and almost fell asleep during the prayers."

"You need a long sleep this afternoon."

He squeezed her hand. "I'll be okay."

She laced her fingers within his warm grasp, reluctant to let go of his hand when the song ended.

He remained standing, stifling a yawn while she picked up her purse.

She held out her open palm. "Keys, please."

"Why?"

"Because you're in no condition to drive." She frowned. "Why didn't you sleep in this morning?"

"I slept for a few hours after dawn, and felt okay when I woke at eight." He dug his keys out of his jeans pocket and handed them to her. "No detours via the mountains."

She curved her lips into a slight smile and dropped his keys into her purse. "We're going straight to your house, unless you want to pick up something for lunch on the way?"

"A Vegemite sandwich will do me for lunch. I feel too tired to eat."

"Okay, let's get going. I'm supposed to be meeting Rachel and Kara for lunch at my favorite café."

"Good." He walked beside her to the main door. "That

means the house will be quiet. Can you keep Rachel away for a few hours?"

She nodded. "They can come back to my place after lunch, and you can message me when you wake up."

"Will do."

She queued at the door with Luke, waiting to shake her pastor's hand before heading out into the bright spring sunshine.

They shuffled forward, crossing the threshold at the entrance to the church.

Amy's father was their pastor, and he shook her hand before gaping at Luke. "What have you done to yourself? You look beyond exhausted."

Luke shrugged, shaking his pastor's outstretched hand. "Work has been full-on."

The pastor furrowed his brows. "Is it okay if I book a time to see you this week for a pastoral visit that's long overdue?"

"Sure." Luke rubbed the back of his hand over his eyes. "Call Janice and book a time that suits you."

"I will." He turned to Megan. "Are you driving him home?"

"Yes, before he falls asleep standing up." She reached for Luke's hand and led him away from the crowd gathered outside the church. "Did you park in your usual spot?"

"I think so."

She located his Jeep in the parking lot and made herself comfortable in the driver's seat.

He reclined the passenger seat and stretched out his legs. "You got what you wanted."

"It would have been nice if it was under better circumstances." She bit her lip. "I'm worried about you. Do you ever take a chunk of time off work?"

He yawned, covering his mouth with his hand. "The clinic is always busy, and my patients don't take a vacation from being sick."

"Couldn't you get Emily or someone to fill in?"

"It isn't as easy as you think to find a replacement, and Emily already has a busy job at the hospital."

"I'm glad you're taking more weekends off from the hospital."

He grinned. "I'm looking forward to our cycling day trip in a couple of weeks."

"It's been too long since I've done a long ride in the mountains."

"It'll be fun."

She drove the short distance to Luke and Rachel's home, liking the feel of the Jeep. She could get used to driving his car.

He led her into his house and headed straight for the sofa. "I'm just going to sit for a minute."

"Sure, I'll fix your sandwich."

She located fresh bread in the kitchen and made his sandwich. Minutes later she entered the quiet living room. Luke was sprawled full length on the sofa, his eyelids shut and breathing shallow. His face relaxed as he lay curled up on his side, a smattering of whiskers covering his unshaven jaw.

She placed his jacket over his shoulders and torso before draping a light blanket over his legs. He pulled the jacket closer to his body, a faint smile on his full lips. He looked settled for at least a few hours.

Megan returned to the kitchen and covered his sandwich with plastic wrap. The camp last weekend plus his rigorous work schedule had wiped him out. She frowned, hoping he wasn't getting sick.

He wasn't the only one who needed to reconsider their

work schedule. Bruce was anxious for an answer on the research position. She didn't know if she was prepared to drag herself away from Luke and her new life in Snowgum Creek.

Chapter 10

Luke slowed his cycling speed and sipped water from his bottle. The midmorning sun scorched his bare arms and legs, the weather unseasonably hot for this early in spring. He swiped beads of sweat off his brow, his hair damp under his bike helmet. Megan rode ahead, her fitted T-shirt clinging to her back as she powered along the winding road.

A herd of brumbies galloped through the pine forest on the high side of the road. The wild horses raced up the hill, weaving around the pine trees. Apple orchards sloped down from the other side of the road, providing a picturesque view of the valley heading back toward Snowgum Creek.

The road ahead straightened out for a long uphill stretch. Megan braked, riding onto the dusty shoulder of the road and coming to a halt under a pine tree. He caught up to her, his breathing ragged.

She smiled. "We picked a hot day."

"Yep." He gulped down a big mouthful of water. "I think we're in for a hot, dry summer."

She held her bottle next to her red-tinged cheek, cooling her face. "I'm glad we set out early. How far are we from the waterfall?"

"About ten miles. The trees will filter the sun once we're deeper in the pine forest."

"That's a relief." She took off her wraparound sunglasses and wiped the lenses with the hem of her T-shirt. "We don't need sunstroke."

"Did you still want to race to the crest of the hill?"

"Of course." Her deep blue eyes sparkled, tiny wrinkles forming in the outer corners as she squinted in the sunlight. "We always race each other on the straight uphill stretches."

"Okay." He had no hope of beating her, and she knew it. "Can we rest here for a few minutes first?"

"Are you tired already?"

He shook his head. "I'm remembering how grueling this hill is on my quads."

"You'll be fine. It's not like it's a vertical slope."

"No, but it's a deceptively gentle-looking hill that goes on forever."

She slipped her sunglasses on her nose and straddled her bike. "How about I give you a head start."

"No way." He stashed his water bottle in the holder on his bike. "You can beat me fair and square, with no concessions." He carried their picnic lunch in a cooler bag strapped to the back of his bike. He'd feel the extra weight on the hill, including their spare bottles of water for the ride home.

"Are you ready?"

He nodded. "Let's do it."

For the first couple of miles he matched her pedal speed, maintaining a brisk pace. He sucked in deep breaths, his body demanding the extra oxygen as the altitude gradually increased. Megan looked as if she was cruising, her streamlined body meshing with her bike as she pushed through the hill climb.

The minutes ticked by and his leg muscles burned from the lactic acid buildup. Megan inched ahead, her endurance outclassing him. Years ago he'd had a chance of beating her to the finish, but her current standard of fitness was superior to his on all levels.

He dropped down another gear, cycling in a standing position to maximize his muscle power. The never-ending hill continued to taunt him, the signpost for the turnoff to the waterfall finally coming into view.

Megan reached the post first, coming to a stop by the side of the road. She tipped her head back, drinking from her water bottle and splashing a handful of water on her face. Perspiration glistened on the exposed skin of her lower arms and legs.

He pulled up beside her, ready to throw his bike away and collapse in the dirt. His legs felt like jelly, spent from the exertion of the hill climb. He planted unsteady feet on the ground, and took a big swig from his water bottle. His body was soaked in sweat and he drank his fill, replenishing his fluid levels. Why had he agreed to this ride? It was going to annihilate him before the day was over.

Megan rolled her shoulders and stretched out her arms. "How are you feeling?"

"You don't want to know."

She laughed, her melodic tone a pleasant balm for his aching body. "It's all downhill now to the creek."

"That's a good thing because I'm not capable of climbing any more hills."

"You'll recover soon, and your warm muscles will feel invigorated."

"Until tomorrow morning, when I'll be stiff and sore."

"Stop worrying about tomorrow. You're missing out on the joy of living in the moment."

"I'm sorry to disappoint you, but right now I'm not feeling joyful."

"You'll get over it. I think you've gone soft in your old age."

He shoved his hands on his hips. "Hey, you're not that far behind me as far as being old is concerned!"

"Well, prove it. Cruise the next few miles down to the creek and we'll have a couple of hours to rest before we need to head home."

"A good plan." The thought of sitting down appealed to him. Plus two uninterrupted hours in her company was a bonus.

They rode in tandem, dodging potholes in the rutted dirt track by staying in the grooves created by the vehicles driven off-road. The waterfall was one of his favorite places, the pristine water flowing through the rugged terrain on its way down the mountains to the township of Snowgum Creek. The melting snowcaps kept the creek running through most of summer, and kayakers enjoyed battling the white-water rapids farther upstream.

He smiled as the sandy basin beside the creek came into view. They had the watering hole to themselves, the gentle rapids and occasional birdsong breaking the silence.

Megan hopped off her bike, wheeling it over to a solid pine tree trunk and resting it out of the sun. She unpacked a picnic blanket and slung her backpack over her shoulders. "Where do we want to park ourselves?"

He pointed to a towering gum tree near the creek, the foliage shading the ground below. "Over there."

"Sounds good." She removed her bike helmet, loosened her ponytail and walked beside him to the tree.

They settled on the picnic blanket in the shade. He ran his fingers through his damp hair, inhaling the fresh pine and eucalyptus scents from the surrounding trees. This part of the creek was a popular swimming spot in summer for those game enough to trek along the long bumpy track.

Megan sat beside him, peeling off her shoes and socks. "The water looks good."

"Yep." He stretched out his legs, thankful they weren't cramping after the arduous ride.

She stashed her sunglasses and wristwatch in her backpack. "I'm going to cool my feet in the water. Are you coming?"

"Not yet." He leaned back, resting his weight on the palms of his hands. "My legs need a break for a bit."

"Okay." She flipped her hair over her shoulders and walked barefoot to the water's edge, twenty feet away. Her feet sank into the sand, and she faced the waterfall upstream.

A light breeze rustled through the leaves overhead, mingling with the soothing rush of water over the falls. He took off his sunglasses, content to let his worries fade away as he enjoyed the tranquility of their peaceful surroundings.

Megan stepped into the creek, the water lapping her ankles.

"Is the water cold?"

"Not really." She turned toward him, wisps of hair blowing across her face. "It's lovely and refreshing."

He nodded. She never used to feel the chill in the water when she was younger, either.

She waded into the water, knee-deep. "I feel like a swim."

His eyebrows shot up. "Fully clothed?"

"Why not? My clothes are already soaked."

He stood. "You're crazy."

"I know." She dived into the water, her body creating a ripple on the surface. Her head emerged in the middle of the creek, and she wiped her hair off her face.

He removed his shoes and socks before heading to the

water's edge. She swam in the middle of the creek on her back, her toes poking out in the water.

His warm feet tingled in the chilly water. "It's freezing."

"No, it's not." She swam closer, a wide smile lighting up her face. "You won't feel the cold once you get in."

He shook his head, stepping deeper into the crystal-clear water. "It's not hot enough to entice me to jump in."

"You have gone soft. Remember how we used to always swim here?"

"In the middle of summer." He lowered his hands into the stream, flicking the refreshing water on his face and arms. "You're not going to talk me into jumping in."

She laughed and swam within six feet of him. "There's more than one way to get you wet."

"Oh, really." He stepped back. "I'm getting out."

She dived back, her fast-kicking legs showering him with icy water.

"Not fair." He waded into the thigh-deep water, the bottom of his shorts ballooning below the surface.

She treaded water and swam closer to shore. "Don't you feel better now?"

"I will soon." He scooped a large handful of water on the surface and fired it in her direction.

Water showered over her face and she rubbed her hand over her eyes. "Water fight."

He flung more water and she retaliated, soaking his T-shirt. Within minutes he gave in, plunging into the water and chasing her to the center of the creek.

She grinned. "I knew I'd get you in the water."

He shook his head, water droplets flying in all directions as he treaded water to stay afloat. "I'm hungry, and I'm getting out now to prepare lunch."

She swam closer. "Is the water too cold?"

He reached out and trailed his fingers along her cheek-bone. "You'll catch a cold if you stay in much longer."

Her eyes widened. "Yes, Doctor."

"You should listen to me."

"Whatever." She placed her hand on his shoulder. "I'll dunk you instead."

"You'll have to catch me first. Race you back." He swam toward the shore, the weight of his T-shirt and shorts slowing his progress. She might be able to outcycle him, but he was no slouch in the water. He cruised to shore a long way ahead of her.

He stood on the sandy bank, a triumphant smile tugging at his mouth. She made her way to the shore, her clothes clinging to her curves.

He drew in a deep breath, averting his gaze and walking back to their picnic blanket. He needed to focus on preparing their lunch instead of being distracted by her stunning natural beauty.

Megan staggered out of the creek, water dripping everywhere. The cool breeze ruffled the ends of her hair as she walked over to Luke.

He crouched beside his bag, retrieving two towels and throwing one in her direction.

"Thanks." She squeezed the excess water out of her hair, creating small puddles at her feet. She must look terrible, her hair stringy and clothes out of shape. At least he was used to seeing her at her worst, all hot and sweaty after a workout.

He rubbed his towel over his hair. "Are you ready to eat?"

She nodded. "Our clothes should dry fast."

"Yep. This sports fabric is great."

"Don't you feel better now after cooling off?"

"Okay, you win that one."

"And the cycling challenge."

He sat on the picnic blanket, legs outstretched and feet facing the water. "But I can still beat you in the pool."

"I'm impressed you're still really fast in the water. Do you train?"

He shook his head. "I find swimming relaxing, and it's good to be left alone in the pool with no interruptions." He reached for a cooler bag, removing two ice bricks and several food containers.

She settled beside him, her knee inches from his leg as she sat cross-legged. "What did you bring?"

He smiled, holding a small bag of crusty French bread rolls. "Ham, Swiss cheese, coleslaw and tabouleh."

"Sounds perfect." She picked up a plate and started adding fillings to a bread roll.

He placed a small bottle of locally produced apple juice beside her knee. "Is this still your favorite?"

She nodded. "Thanks. I can't buy this brand in Sydney."

"You miss out on all the good stuff in Sydney."

"I like living in Sydney. You can't deny the harbor and beaches are gorgeous."

"Yes, but Sydney doesn't have this." He waved his hand in the direction of the waterfall. "Fresh mountain air, ski fields nearby. What more could you want?"

"Don't forget the Blue Mountains are pretty."

"Did you visit there often? I know I didn't when I lived in Sydney."

"No, but I did occasionally cycle in the national parks that were closer to my apartment."

He unwrapped a Vegemite sandwich, cut into two triangles. "For you."

She laughed. "You remembered."

"Of course." His warm gaze connected with hers. "How could I forget our tradition?"

Her heart skipped a beat, memories of shared picnics in Snowgum Creek and Sydney filling her mind. "It wouldn't be a picnic without a Vegemite sandwich."

"And I'm no longer a poor struggling student. I can afford to splash out at the deli and buy something more exotic than Vegemite."

She reached for her half of the sandwich. "Thanks for bringing lunch."

"You're welcome." He made up two rolls, overflowing with ham, cheese and coleslaw.

"You're not having tabouleh."

"I bought it especially for you."

"Thank you. I'm impressed you remembered I like it with ham."

"I remember a lot of things."

His statement hung in the air, a poignant reminder of how he knew her better than most people. Why had she let him go? Her twenty-one-year-old self hadn't appreciated his thoughtfulness, and she had cast his love aside for new adventures. If she could relive that moment when he'd proposed marriage at dusk on Balmoral Beach in Sydney, would she have a different answer now?

Megan breathed in the serenity of her surroundings as they ate their lunch. Her body relaxed and she stretched out her legs. Her muscles had recovered and she was prepared for the long downhill ride home.

She finished eating her roll and packed away her plate. Luke had polished off his rolls in record time.

She turned her head toward him, staring deep into his golden eyes. "That was delicious."

He held her gaze, his eyes softening.

She flicked a few damp locks of hair back over her shoulders, her T-shirt and cycling shorts already dry.

He planted his hand on the blanket behind her and she rested back against his shoulder, a comfortable position reminiscent of previous picnics.

She sipped the remains of her apple juice. "I'd forgotten how much I love it here."

"Me, too." His head almost touched hers and he turned toward her, his breath warm on her ear. "Have I told you how beautiful you are?"

She sucked in a deep breath, her pulse rate accelerating. His words awakened responses she hadn't experienced since she'd left him years ago. "Not today."

His fingers caressed her cheek, tucking a few loose strands of hair behind her ears. "You always look stunning."

"Hardly." She giggled. "My hair is a disaster, and frizzy after the swim."

He shook his head, his fingers entwined in her hair at the nape of her neck. "Your hair is lovely."

She leaned toward him, her eyes locked in his intense gaze. "I've missed this. You and me together, like old times."

"Yes." His eyes darkened, and the hand entangled in her hair drew her head closer. "We shared some memorable moments."

She closed her eyes and his lips brushed over hers, soft and inviting. She sighed and traced her fingertips over his jaw and neck. She parted her lips and he deepened the kiss. He wrapped his arm around her waist.

She twined her fingers in his hair, inhaling his distinctive male scent intermingled with traces of aftershave. The past eight years evaporated as a torrent of old emotions swept over her. Time suspended and she became lost in his arms, her hand gripping his broad shoulder.

He lifted his head, breaking their connection. "Wow."

She opened her eyes, pressing her fingers to her lips. What was she going to do about the research job? How could she contemplate leaving him a second time?

Chapter 11

Luke rested his hands on Megan's shoulders, his gaze taking in her flushed face and full lips. He drew her close and she snuggled in his arms, her head tucked under his chin. The gum tree overhead rustled in the breeze, and the afternoon sun shimmered on the rippling water in the creek.

His mind replayed their incredible kiss, and his growing yearning for another one. It felt right to be sitting with her on the picnic blanket. He held her in his arms, inhaling the floral scent in her hair. She'd reignited old feelings that he'd thought were gone forever. He'd dreamed about this moment, could hardly believe it was real. She'd returned to him and Snowgum Creek.

She stirred and pulled back, putting a few inches of distance between them. "What are we doing?"

He grinned. "Isn't it obvious?"

She nibbled her lower lip. "Is this a good idea?"

He widened his eyes. "We've been tiptoeing around the whole dating issue since our dinner at the Chinese restaurant."

"I know, but I'm not sure what I'm doing next year."

He cupped her chin in his hand. "You have a few options for staying in Snowgum Creek, and your personal training business is starting to gain some traction."

"Yes, but I can't make any promises."

"I'm not asking for any." He dropped a kiss on her lips. "We have plenty of time before you need to make any decisions."

She lowered her lashes. "I don't know."

"What do you think is going to happen? It's not like you've already decided to leave." Maybe he was premature to believe she was ready to settle and put down roots. He'd let her go once and, now they'd reconnected, he didn't want to think about the possibility that she might leave again.

She shook her head. "I have options but I don't know what I want to do. My business isn't doing as well as I'd hoped."

"It takes time to build a business, and your hospital contract has a number of months to go." He reached for her hand. "We can see how things evolve and not rush into making any decisions." Why was she hedging? Had he read the situation wrong?

"I don't want to hurt you again."

He laced his fingers in hers. "We're not kids anymore, and we're mature enough to have a rational conversation and discuss our options together."

Her mouth gaped open. "I'm not good at this joint-decision thing."

"We can pray about it, and ask that God will open up the right career opportunities for you."

"Yes, prayer would be helpful."

He draped his arm over her shoulders and stared at the waterfall. Could he risk his heart again, knowing what had happened last time?

Lord, I don't know what Your plans are, but I really care about Megan and I want to explore the possibility of a future with her.

Three days later, Megan made two lattes in the staff room at the clinic. She'd spent most of the afternoon cleaning her cottage and worrying about her lack of appointments that week. She'd arranged to meet Luke at the clinic after he finished his afternoon patient list. Business was slowing down, and she really needed to pick up more clients soon to maintain its financial viability.

She placed the steaming mugs on the table and Luke strolled into the room, a beaming smile on his handsome face.

"Hi, gorgeous." He snuck a kiss on her lips.

Her heartbeat quickened, the old nickname bringing back fond memories. "Perfect timing. I just made our coffee."

"Thank you." He slouched in a seat beside her, unbuttoning the cuffs of his shirt and rolling up the sleeves.

"Have you had a busy day?"

He nodded. "Amy went home early because one of the kids had something on at school, and I picked up a couple of her patients this afternoon."

She sipped her latte, the strong brew bringing a smile to her lips. "You work too hard."

"I know." He cradled his coffee mug between his hands. "But I'm taking this weekend off, from noon on Saturday."

Her smile widened. "I'm glad you're not on call at the hospital."

"Me, too. Are you working here on Saturday?"

She shook her head. "I have a few clients at the gym, then I'm heading out to see Jack and Kate for lunch and my parents for dinner. You're invited to both."

"Okay. Is there any chance we can see your parents at lunch?"

"Nope. They're heading out of town to visit friends. Why?"

His eyes lit up. "I was hoping to take you out to dinner."

She held his warm gaze. "Really?"

He grinned. "Somewhere swish."

"Sounds great. We can go on Friday night."

"Don't I have youth group?"

"Not this week because of the school holidays."

He raised an eyebrow. "How come you seem to know more about my schedule than I do?"

She chuckled. "I got lucky. Rachel and Kara were talking about youth group at church on Sunday night."

"That makes sense. Do you have plans with them on Friday?"

"Nothing that can't be changed. By the way, Rachel is cooking dinner for us and Kara tonight."

"That's good news. She's been experimenting with a few delicious new recipes." He stretched his arms out over his head. "We can drive over to my place now."

"That works for me."

"So, we have a date for Friday night? I'll take you somewhere really nice in Sunny Ridge."

"Sounds intriguing. Why Sunny Ridge?"

"Because I'll have half a chance of keeping you to myself without constant interruptions."

"True." The Snowgum Creek residents tended to stop by their table when they went out to a restaurant in town. A little bit more anonymity in Sunny Ridge would be a nice change. "What should I wear?"

"Something suitable for fine dining."

"Oh, we are going somewhere swish."

He laughed. "Only the best for my girl."

Her phone chimed in her purse. She checked the caller ID. Bruce. "I need to take this call."

"Sure."

She answered the call and walked out into the empty reception area.

"Megan, I'm glad I caught you," Bruce said.

"What can I do for you?"

"Give me an answer on the research position. I thought you were keen to take on the project next year."

She tightened her grip on her phone. "I'm still working through a few details."

Bruce paused. "I can find someone else, if you don't want to do it."

"No, I'm interested but I'm not sure if I can make it work with my other commitments."

"I need a definite yes or no by Monday at the absolute latest."

"Sure." She had five days to work out what she wanted to do. "I promise I'll get back to you by Monday."

"Good. I have to lodge all the preliminary research information next week to finalize the funding arrangements. They need to know who will be the principal researchers for the project."

"I understand."

"If you say yes, your decision needs to be firm."

She cringed. "That's why I'm not rushing my decision."

"Megan, I'd really like to work with you on this project. It would be an excellent career move for you, and probably lead to overseas research opportunities."

She squirmed. "I know, and I do appreciate the opportunity and your support. I'll be in touch." She ended the call and returned to the staff room.

Luke rinsed his coffee mug in the sink. "Is everything okay?"

"Yes, just a work call."

"A new client?"

"Unfortunately, no." Her stomach churned, the reality of her impending decision imploding her mind.

Lord, I'm confused and conflicted over this decision. I don't think it's possible to have a relationship with Luke and take on the research job. I don't know if I'm prepared to decline such an incredible career opportunity, but I can't bear the thought of leaving Luke again, either.

On Friday morning Luke sat forward in his leather chair beside Kate in his room at the clinic. He wound the blood pressure cuff around her upper arm.

Kate smiled. "I hope my blood pressure is still normal."

He nodded. "You're doing very well, and now that you're thirty-eight weeks you don't have long to go."

"I wonder if the baby will come early or late."

"Who knows?" He pumped air into the cuff. "Your baby will make an appearance when he or she is ready. Have you packed your bag for the hospital?"

"Yes, it's sitting next to the door. Jack's making sure my car is topped up with fuel, just in case we have to drive to Sunny Ridge in the middle of the night."

"A good plan." He let out the air in the cuff, his attention focused on the monitor. "All good. The hot weather hasn't affected your blood pressure."

"That's good news. My ankles are a little bit swollen, but otherwise I'm feeling okay."

He placed the stethoscope on Kate's swollen belly. "The baby's heartbeat is strong."

Kate let out a deep breath. "I'm so glad to hear this. Bub has been less active over the last few days."

"The baby has dropped into a lower position in preparation for the birth, but you need to make sure you can still feel some movement."

She nodded. "I'm paying close attention."

"Good. Do you want to hear the heartbeat?"

"Yes, please." Kate took hold of the stethoscope, slipping the earbuds into her ears. "Wow, it sounds really loud."

He smiled. "Your baby is doing well."

"I'm so excited."

"Me, too." He typed a few sentences on Kate's file in his computer. "We're done for today. Can you please make an appointment with Janice for next week?"

"Sure." She stood, stretching out her back. "I'm looking forward to being able to walk again instead of waddling."

He laughed. "You're doing great. I'll let your obstetrician know everything is on track."

"Thanks, Luke."

"You're welcome."

He clicked out of Kate's file, checking his appointment list in his online calendar.

"I'm supposed to be meeting Megan. Is she around?"

"I've no idea." He stood and walked with Kate into the reception area. "My schedule has been nonstop for the last few hours."

Megan sat behind the reception desk, chatting with Janice. Her beautiful blue eyes lit up, and she walked over to her friends. "Kate, you're looking great."

Kate smiled. "I thought you'd like this dress."

"Very girlie." Megan turned in his direction, bestowing her megawatt smile on him. "Do you have time for coffee?"

He nodded. "A quick one. I only have ten minutes."

"Sounds good," Megan said.

He followed Megan and Kate into the staff room.

Megan switched on the coffee machine. "Kate, how did your appointment go?"

"Very well. Bub's heartbeat sounds really strong and Luke's happy with my progress."

He nodded. "Kate and the baby are doing well."

"I'm so glad to hear it," Megan said. "I know Jack is starting to fret."

"First-time-father jitters." He grinned. "Megan, I have

good news. I managed to book a table tonight at The Ridge."

"Wow." Megan's eyes widened. "I haven't been there in years."

Kate's jaw dropped. "You're taking Megan to The Ridge? Tonight?"

"I was lucky to snag a cancellation." The Ridge was the best fine-dining restaurant in Sunny Ridge, with incredible views over the township.

Kate tipped her head to the side. "What's the occasion?"

Megan concentrated on making their coffees. "No reason."

"Well, actually, Megan and I are dating."

"Really?" Kate switched her attention to Megan. "I had no idea things between you two had become serious."

Megan handed a coffee mug to Kate. "I was going to tell you at lunch but Luke has beaten me to it."

Kate sipped her coffee. "Does Jack know?"

Luke shook his head. "I haven't had a chance to talk to him this week because work has been crazy busy." He didn't add that he'd spent most of his spare time with Megan.

Kate placed the mug on the table and lowered herself into a chair. "It seems like Megan and I have a lot to talk about over lunch."

He glanced at his watch. "You'll both have to excuse me. I just remembered I need to call the hospital."

"Here's your latte." Megan passed him a mug, the aromatic blend teasing his senses.

"Thanks. Enjoy your lunch." He planted a kiss on Megan's sweet lips before walking back to his office, a new lightness in his step. He had arrangements to make for tonight, and not a lot of time to get organized. He wanted tonight to be perfect.

* * *

Megan leaned forward in her chair opposite Kate in the staff room, sipping her coffee.

Kate sat up straighter, her brows raised. "What's going on? Since when did you and Luke get back together?"

She pressed her lips together. "It only happened on Sunday. We went on a cycling day trip to the waterfall."

"Oh. Why didn't you tell me about your cycling date?"

"Because I didn't want you to make it into a big deal."

Kate sighed. "Of course it's a big deal. Luke doesn't date unless he has serious intentions, and I didn't know you'd decided to stay in Snowgum Creek indefinitely."

"Um, well, I still haven't made up my mind."

Kate crossed her arms on the table, her voice firm. "Please tell me you've told Luke about the research job."

She examined her fingernails, avoiding Kate's penetrating gaze. "Not yet."

"Megan, you can't do this to Luke. How can you start dating him and not tell him you might be leaving next year?"

"I've tried to tell him, but the right opportunity hasn't presented itself."

"Seriously?" Kate sipped her latte. "You have to be honest with him, and tell him what's going on in your head."

"But if I tell him, it's only going to complicate everything. If I turn down the job and he knows nothing about it, then it makes life easier for everyone."

"You can't spend your life running away from conflict."

"I don't do that."

"Yes, you do. Look at the fiasco with Jason following you here. And the way you left Luke and ran away to Canada."

"That's different."

"How? Sometimes you have to initiate the hard conversations. A healthy relationship involves honesty and open communication. Now that you're dating Luke, you need to open up and share all this stuff with him."

She dragged her teeth over her lower lip. "I'm not good at this sharing business."

"Do you trust him?"

Megan nodded.

"Then you have nothing to fear by opening up to him. How do you know he won't be supportive of you taking on the research job?"

Her shoulders slumped. "His life is established here, and the research job is based in Sydney for at least two years."

"Have you made a decision about the job?"

"Not yet. I don't know what I want to do, but I have until Monday to make a decision."

"You need to tell Luke about this research job offer as soon as possible. Tonight would be good." Kate's tone brooked no argument.

Megan's grip tightened on her coffee mug. "Okay. I'll tell him tonight."

Kate's mouth curved up into a half smile. "You won't regret sharing this with him. Luke's a great guy, and I can tell he really cares about you. Together you can find a way forward."

She drank her coffee, contemplating Kate's advice. Her best friend was right. Luke deserved to know about the research job opportunity, even if she ultimately decided to turn the job down. She had to find the courage to open up and share this news with him.

Chapter 12

Megan applied mascara and scrutinized her makeup in her bathroom mirror. She didn't wear a lot of makeup for work, and the black eyeliner brought out the dark blue color of her eyes.

She ran her hands over the fitted skirt of her knee-length sleeveless sapphire-blue dress. A balmy evening with possible storms was forecasted, unusual for this time of year. There were reports of wildfires breaking out in the mountains due to lightning strikes. She was thankful the fires wouldn't affect their drive into Sunny Ridge, the opposite direction from the mountains.

Her doorbell pealed, and she collected her purse on her way to the door. Luke stood on the threshold, immaculately groomed in a pressed pale blue shirt and navy blue suit pants.

His smile broadened. "Wow, you look incredible."

Warmth rose up her neck. "Thanks. You're looking pretty good yourself."

He stepped forward, pressing his lips to hers.

She pulled back. "It's too early in the evening for you to ruin my lipstick."

He laughed. "Your vanity is endearing, but I quite like the just-been-kissed look of smudged lipstick."

She playfully smacked his arm and closed her front door. "Let's get going. I'm looking forward to dinner."

"Me, too." He held her hand and led her to his Jeep.

She negotiated the uneven front path in two-inch heels, glad to have him by her side to help maintain her balance.

He opened the passenger door, and she stepped up into the soft leather seat.

"Thank you." She buckled her seat belt and tucked her hair behind her ears. The humidity had risen as the day progressed, and she lifted her hair off the back of her clammy neck. They'd need to use the air-conditioning during the two-hour drive to Sunny Ridge.

Luke slid into his seat and started the engine. "Did you hear about the fires?"

She nodded. "Thankfully they're not close to us."

"The pine forests are tinder-dry."

"Yep, and there's a faint whiff of smoke in the air."

He bumped up the air-conditioning. "Not for long. We're driving away from the smoke."

Megan chatted with Luke during the drive. She procrastinated, and didn't mention the research job on their journey to the restaurant. Why spoil their dinner with an intense conversation about her future employment? A much better idea to leave that conversation topic for the drive home.

Luke negotiated the light traffic in Sunny Ridge, and headed to the other side of town. They crawled up a winding road to the restaurant, perched at the top of the steep hill with a three-sixty-degree view of the surrounding region. The sunset was imminent, the western sky highlighted by spectacular hues of pink and orange.

Luke pulled into a space in the crowded parking lot, full of top-of-the-line SUVs and luxury cars. The wealthy residents of Sunny Ridge had claimed The Ridge as their preferred dining destination.

He opened her door and helped her down, his grip firm on her hand. "What do you think of the view?"

"It's stunning." The sun was dipping below the horizon, casting a golden glow on the town below. "I hope we have a table with a view."

He smiled. "I requested one, and we'll see what happens."

"Do you know the owners?"

"Yes, and I used to dine here when I lived in Sunny Ridge."

"Why am I surprised? I'll say it again—you could charm anyone."

He twined his fingers with hers. "I don't care about charming anyone else. I just hope I'm charming you."

She nodded, leaning closer into his side. "You're pulling out all the stops tonight."

"We're just getting started." He glanced at her feet. "Can you actually walk in those heels?"

"Of course. Just because I live in running shoes at work doesn't mean I can't walk in heels when the occasion calls for it." Her matching sapphire-blue pumps were a recent addition to her wardrobe.

He laughed. "I'm just checking that I don't need to carry you into the restaurant, since you looked a bit unsteady on your front path."

"Very funny. I'll prove to you that I'm not a klutz in heels."

"Okay." He retrieved his jacket from the backseat.

"Are you cold?"

"No, but the air-conditioning might be cool."

"I didn't think to bring a jacket."

He gave her a brilliant smile. "You can wear mine."

"Thanks for thinking of me." She held his gaze, warmth rising in her cheeks.

"You're welcome." He placed his hand on her waist, and strolled beside her to the restaurant entrance.

The maître d', clad in an elegant tuxedo, greeted them. "Luke Morton, it's good to see you. It's been too long."

Luke shook his hand, his welcome warm. "I don't get out this way very often. John, let me introduce you to my date, Megan Bradley."

John smiled. "Megan, it's lovely to meet you, and I trust you'll have an enjoyable evening. I've reserved a table by a window with a nice view."

"Thank you. That sounds wonderful."

John led them to a table in the lounge area adjacent to the restaurant. A waiter hovered nearby. "Mark will take care of your drinks when you're ready, and I'll be back shortly to escort you to your table."

Luke smiled. "Thanks, John."

"You're welcome." John returned to the restaurant entrance.

Luke pulled out a chair beside the window and she sank into the comfortable seat.

He sat beside her, his fingers entwined in hers. "Does this meet your expectations?"

"Yes, I love the view." Twilight had set in, and the streetlights in Sunny Ridge twinkled below like stars on the inky ground.

He placed their drink order with Mark and lounged back in his seat. "Should I be concerned about dinner with your parents tomorrow night?"

She laughed. "You're not eighteen anymore."

"That's a relief. I remember your father giving me the third degree with a million questions."

"I know. I was so embarrassed, and we got into a big argument after you left."

"Really? You never told me that."

"There wasn't much to tell. He thought I was too young to get into a serious relationship."

"Was he right?"

Mark arrived with their drinks, giving her a moment to compose an answer.

She sipped her iced tea. "I think he knew me better than I knew myself."

"Do you regret our previous relationship?"

She widened her eyes. "Of course not. We had a lot of fun together, and you kept me sane while I lived in Sydney in that horrible dorm."

He shook his head. "I don't know how you got any studying done with those girls around and their constant parties. Did they fail their exams?"

"I can't remember. A few of them dropped out of school. I used to hide in my room, headphones on."

He grinned. "You made good grades. Did you ever think about doing postgraduate studies?"

She sucked in a sharp breath. "Not back then. I was too interested in my annual trek to the ski fields to commit to more study."

"True. Have you missed being at the ski fields this year?"

"Sometimes, but it's been good to do something different."

John reappeared and ushered them to a white-linen-clad table in a secluded corner of the spacious restaurant. All the tables they passed were occupied, and a pianist played a classical piece on a baby grand piano on the far side of the room.

A waiter placed a linen napkin on her lap and handed her a menu. She glanced over the selections, her taste buds inspired by the choices.

Luke sipped his iced water. "What do you feel like?"

She drew her brows together. "I don't know. The barramundi looks interesting."

"It's really good." He closed his menu. "Would you like a starter?"

"Yes, but then I won't have room for dessert."

"That's okay." He reached for her hand, caressing his thumb over her fingertips. "We can have all three courses another time."

Her heart warmed at his words. "Sounds good. I guess we can't stay too long since we have a long drive home tonight."

He shrugged. "We'll see what the night brings. I start work tomorrow at nine."

"Ugh, not fun. My first appointment at the gym isn't until ten."

"Lucky girl, you can sleep in."

"I just might do that." She perused the menu. "The wild mushrooms to start are a possibility."

He wrinkled his nose. "I don't understand why you love mushrooms."

"It's not like I'm going to make you eat them."

"You better not."

"What are you having?"

"Definitely the lobster ravioli to start."

"Is it good?"

He nodded. "My favorite starter."

"And you're having the rib-eye steak."

He grinned. "I'm predictable, but the chef always cooks the beef to perfection, melt in your mouth."

"Sounds great."

A waiter took their order, and before long their starters arrived.

Megan tasted a mushroom. "I'm impressed."

"You wait until you try the barramundi."

"I'm looking forward to it."

The sky had darkened outside and she felt as if they were in their own little world, away from the prying eyes of other guests. "It's nice to have some space."

He ate his last mouthful of ravioli. "This table is in a good position. We can see the other diners but we're not close enough to overhear their conversations."

"I like it." She finished her plate of mushrooms, her stomach replete. "Thank you for bringing me here tonight. It means a lot to me."

He reached into his jacket pocket, slung over the back of his chair. "I have something for you." He placed a small envelope and a rectangle-shaped jewelry box on the table.

"Oh, Luke, what is it?"

His smile lit up his eyes. "You'll have to open it up."

She undid the gold ribbon around the navy blue box. She lifted the lid and gasped. A sapphire-and-gold bracelet lay on a velvet casing, the stones flashing in the restaurant's muted lighting.

"Wow." She lifted the bracelet out of the box. "This is stunning and matches my necklace and earrings."

"I'm glad you like it."

"I love it." She secured the bracelet around her wrist, holding her hand up to examine the intricate gold setting around each stone. "This is gorgeous."

"A beautiful gift for a beautiful woman."

"You're spoiling me."

He grinned. "That's the plan."

She opened the envelope and removed a small card. She squinted, trying to decipher the words. "I can barely read your handwriting. Does it say 'to a special woman'?"

"To a sensational woman."

"Oh, that makes sense." His handwriting was still dreadful, and harder to read now than it was years ago.

He brushed his lips over her hand, sending tingles up her arm. "It's the truth." .

Her pulse raced, his words thrilling and scaring her all at once. Their relationship was rolling forward faster than she'd anticipated, but she was determined to enjoy every minute of his company.

Their next course arrived. She inhaled the pleasant aroma of his hearty beef dish mingling with the tropical scents from her barramundi fillet.

"Wow." She picked up her cutlery. "This looks and smells marvelous."

He nodded. "Wait until you taste it."

The fish fillet fell apart as she scooped a portion on her fork. The delicious flavors burst open on her tongue. She sighed. "This is sensational. A unique combination of ingredients that works."

He cut into his juicy steak, cooked medium with a pink strip in the middle. "I've never once been disappointed by a course here."

"I can understand why. The food is top-notch."

"Is it as good as your posh city food?"

"Possibly better." She grinned. "I love the freshness and the quality of the produce."

"Have you changed your mind about dessert?"

She shook her head. "I'll be full after this course, but don't let me stop you from indulging if you feel like something sweet."

He nodded. "I'll settle for coffee to keep me awake for the drive home."

"A good idea." She relaxed back in her seat and slowly ate her meal, savoring the delicate flavors. The food was nutritious, and the barramundi tasted as though it had been steamed with the fruit and spices. Kudos to the chef. She was adept in the kitchen, but she did struggle to cook fish the way she liked it.

He finished his steak, a satisfied expression on his face. "That was excellent."

A hovering waiter cleared their plates and Luke ordered coffee.

She glanced at her watch. If they left soon, they'd be back in Snowgum Creek by eleven.

She stared at her bracelet, admiring the quality of the stones. It wasn't a cheap gift and she understood the intent behind it. Kate was right. Luke had serious intentions, and it wasn't looking as though he would waste any time chasing after what he wanted.

A lump caught in her throat. She was in way deeper than she'd anticipated at the start of the evening. How could she possibly tell him about the research job offer after the time and energy he had invested in making this evening special for both of them?

Their coffee arrived and she sipped the smooth brew. A perfect way to end their dinner.

Luke looked past her shoulder, his eyes narrowed. "Bruce from the hospital is heading our way."

She coughed, nearly choking on her coffee. This couldn't be happening. Not tonight, when she and Luke were finally in a good place.

Bruce appeared beside her. A young, pretty blonde hung on to his arm. "Hello, Megan, Luke. You've traveled a long way for dinner tonight."

Luke nodded, his mouth set in a grim line. "The food and ambience is worth it. What can we do for you? I assume there's a reason you've stopped by."

Megan's gaze darted between Luke and Bruce, the tension between the two men palpable. Her stomach churned. There was obviously a history between them that wasn't good.

Bruce switched his attention to her. "I'm waiting on Megan to give me an answer."

The blonde giggled. "Why? What's going on?"

Bruce gave her an indulgent smile. "It's work-related, sweetheart."

Luke's piercing gaze settled on Megan. "What answer?"

Megan gulped. "I was going to tell you—"

"Tell me what?" Luke crossed his arms over his chest.

Bruce smirked. "I've offered Megan a master's research position for a skiing project starting in July next year, based in Sydney. I need a definite answer by Monday."

Chapter 13

Luke clenched his jaw, counting to ten. He looked Megan straight in the eye, his tone terse. "Do you have an answer for Bruce?"

Megan dug her teeth into her lip and lowered her lashes. "Not yet."

Bruce grunted. "I need an answer by nine on Monday morning."

"Okay." Her gaze remained focused on her coffee cup. "I'll be in touch."

The blonde woman accompanying Bruce tugged on his arm and pouted. "We're going to be late for the movie."

Bruce nodded. "Enjoy your evening." He walked away, the blonde clinging to him as she stumbled in her stiletto heels.

Megan clasped her hands together, not meeting Luke's gaze.

Luke let out a big breath. "Do you have anything to say?"

She looked up, her beautiful blue eyes glassy. "I don't know what to say."

"How long have you known about the research opportunity?"

She flinched, his question hanging in the air for a long moment. "A while."

Luke bit back a harsh retort, adrenaline pumping

through his body. Divorced and in his late thirties, Bruce was a former colleague at Sunny Ridge Hospital who had a reputation as a player. The look in Bruce's eye had suggested he was interested in Megan on a personal as well as professional level.

Megan covered her face with her hands. "I know I've messed up."

Her words impaled his heart like a sharp blade. Why couldn't she trust him? Was it that hard for her to find the courage to confide in him?

"Does Kate know about the job offer?"

She nodded.

"And Emily?"

"Yes, I was going to tell you—"

"When? After you'd decided to accept the job offer? Or were you going to decline the offer and pretend it never happened?"

She sat up straighter, seeming to pull herself together. "Can we talk about this later?"

He threw his hands in the air. "Of course, why did I possibly think you'd be interested in communicating with me?" He signaled a waiter and finalized their bill with his credit card.

Megan dabbed a finger at the corner of her eye. "I need to visit the bathroom before we leave."

He nodded and stood. "The bathrooms are near the entrance. We can meet at the front door."

He walked behind her, taking in a few calming breaths. Her refusal to confide in him had wounded him in ways he'd never envisaged. He thought they'd established a strong friendship, and the foundation for a relationship based on trust and honesty. How could she keep this opportunity a secret?

"Why didn't you say something?"

She closed her eyes. "I'd never really thought about pursuing an academic career. I love skiing and my regular job each season at the ski resort. This research project is my ideal job and it could lead to opportunities overseas."

"Combining sports science and skiing."

"Yep. A once-in-a-lifetime opportunity. Bruce is very keen to bring me on board."

"I noticed his interest in you."

"Purely professional, of course. He's a respected sports medicine doctor, and working on a collaborative project with him would boost my career."

He groaned. "I know his reputation."

"It's not like that, Luke. He hasn't been sleazy or anything."

"Okay, if you say so." He overtook a slow truck on the highway. "Are you happy in Snowgum Creek?"

"Yes, I've loved coming home and feeling like I belong in a small community. I've missed this over the years, and I like my work. The downside is my business is slow."

"What do you really want? Is a career important? Do you want to chase the big sports science research career?"

"Yes and no. That's the thing. I can't decide what I want to do."

"Why didn't you tell me about this earlier?" He ran his fingers through his hair. "I could have tried to help you work through this decision."

"But you have a stake in this, too." She suppressed a sigh. "If I leave, it would be hard to continue our relationship."

"You won't consider a long-distance relationship?"

"If I chase a research career, I want the freedom to travel and work overseas. Your life is established here in Snowgum Creek."

He tapped his fingers on the steering wheel. "And Bruce needs an answer by Monday morning."

"I have the weekend to work out what I want to do."

"One more question." He cleared his throat. "When were you planning to tell me about all this?"

Her heart constricted. "Tonight, after dinner."

"Really?"

"I was working up the courage to tell you when Bruce turned up at our table."

"How do I know you're telling the truth?"

"You can ask Kate. I promised her this afternoon that I'd tell you tonight."

"There's one thing I don't get." He paused, his voice low. "Why don't you trust me?"

"I do trust you."

"You have a funny way of showing it. Here's the thing. I can't pursue a relationship with you if you think it's okay to keep this kind of stuff from me."

She gulped. "Are you breaking up with me?"

"No, I'm telling you my expectations. Honest and open communication, working together to make joint decisions, and no secrets. These aren't negotiable."

She pressed her fingers to her temples, her head pounding. "Can we talk more tomorrow? I need time to think and pray."

"I can swing by Jack and Kate's place after I visit Ben's farm for a late lunch."

"Okay. That works for me. Do you still want to have dinner with my parents?"

"Yes. I can't pretend I'm not disappointed that you didn't share this with me. But I do want to support you." His tone softened. "And I'll be praying for you."

"Thanks." The sincerity in his voice gave her hope. She planned to go home and open her Bible. The special

Bible that Luke had given her years ago. Could she find the answers to her current dilemma? Sleep would likely be elusive. Her Monday-morning deadline loomed like a storm cloud ready to burst in her mind.

Megan carried a coffee tray outside and joined Kate on the back deck. She'd enjoyed a lovely lunch with Jack and Kate, and her brother had left them alone to chat. Kate wanted to enjoy their coffee outdoors.

A strong aroma of smoke infused the air, a brown haze covering the orchards in the distance.

Megan frowned. "Do you want to go back inside? The smoke is getting thicker."

"No, I'm restless and sick of being indoors." Kate stood in front of her chair, stretching her back muscles. "We can move if the wind changes direction."

She poured their coffee, adding milk and sugar. "I wonder if any new fires have flared up."

Kate settled back in her seat. "Who knows? Anyway, have you made a decision? Did you tell Luke about the research job?"

Megan handed Kate a mug of coffee and filled her in with all the important details about her eventful night out with Luke.

Kate's jaw dropped. "You certainly know how to make everything so much worse."

"Don't remind me." She scrutinized her fingernails. "I regret not listening to you and Emily."

"What are you going to do about the job offer? You're running out of time to make a decision."

She tasted her coffee, too weak for her liking. "I'm torn between chasing my dream career and wanting to stay here with Luke."

"Do you love Luke?"

Her heart squeezed tight in her chest. "I've always loved Luke, even after I left last time." She stared out at the orchards, the brown smoke haze dominating the horizon. "I haven't met anyone who compares to Luke."

"I can highly recommend married life." Kate sipped her milky coffee. "The best thing I ever did was stay here and marry Jack."

"But you weren't turning your back on a great career. I don't want to settle for life with Luke and live with a whole bunch of regrets."

"Do you regret leaving him last time?"

She shook her head. "I do regret the way I did it. I was too immature to even contemplate the idea of marriage, and all I had wanted to do was travel."

"You're older and wiser now, and you've traveled the world." Kate wriggled in her seat. "Are you sure you want the big career, at the expense of marriage and children?"

Megan rubbed her hands over her face. "I don't know. Could I be happy living indefinitely in Snowgum Creek? I already have itchy feet to travel. I don't know if I'm capable of being the wife that Luke is hoping to marry."

Kate sat forward in her seat, arching her back. "Has he talked about marriage?"

"Not exactly, but I know where his head is, and he's not going to waste any time."

"Ouch." Kate stood. "I think I need to walk around for a bit."

"Are you okay?"

She paced along the veranda. "Is Jack still in the house?"

"I think so. Doris stopped by while I was making our coffee." Megan widened her eyes, covering her mouth with her hand. "Are you in labor?"

"Maybe." Kate placed her hands on her stomach, her

flat sandals clunking on the wooden decking. "I think I'm having contractions."

"I'll find Jack."

"The pain is getting intense."

Megan ran into the house. "Jack, where are you?"

Jack jogged down the hall, his brows drawn into a straight line. "What's wrong?"

"Kate thinks she's in labor."

"What?" His mouth gaped open. "The roads are blocked with the fires."

"Which roads?"

"All the main routes to Sunny Ridge. A new fire has started near Snowgum Creek, and the roads into town are closed."

"Call Luke. He should be at Ben's farm unless he is stuck in town."

"Okay, I'll find my phone. Can you stay with Kate?"

"Yes." Megan handed him her phone. "Luke's on my speed dial."

"Thanks."

She raced back outside to Kate. "How are you doing?"

Kate ambled along the deck, massaging one side of her swollen abdomen. "This baby is coming."

"Jack is calling Luke now. Can I get you anything?"

"My hospital bag is packed and ready beside the back door."

"Do you think you'll need to go there this afternoon?"

Kate nodded. "The contractions are strong and closer together. Bub is getting ready to make an appearance."

Megan sucked in a deep breath. How were they going to get Kate to Sunny Ridge Hospital in time if all the roads were closed?

Chapter 14

Luke rested his hands on the edge of Ben's kitchen counter, staring out the window at the smoke plume building on the horizon. "The fire is looking really close."

Ben chopped up a range of vegetables from his garden at his kitchen island. "It's in the pine forest and it looks like you're stuck out here. The roads back into town are now closed."

He turned around and walked over to the kitchen island. "It's a good thing I'm meeting Megan at Jack's farm."

Ben paused, a wide grin covering his face. "Are things getting serious between you two?"

"Maybe." He rubbed his hand over his jaw. "Everything was going great until she dropped her bomb last night."

"What did she do this time?"

"I found out from Bruce that he has offered her a research position on his new skiing project."

"What? How did you have the misfortune of running into Bruce?"

"I took Megan to The Ridge last night."

Ben let out a low whistle. "You really are serious about Megan. Why didn't she tell you about her new job opportunity?"

"Long story, and she hasn't made a decision yet. Bruce expects an answer from her by Monday morning."

Ben scraped a pile of diced vegetables into his slow cooker. "What does this mean for your relationship with Megan? She'd better not ditch you a second time."

He shoved his hands on his hips. "This time if we split it's not going to be because she ran away and we didn't have a chance to talk through the issues."

"Is she opening up more?"

"I had thought so, but now I'm not so sure."

Ben started peeling a carrot. "I'll pray for you, bro. It sounds like you're in for a full-on weekend."

"Yeah. So much for relaxing and taking a break." His phone rang and he checked the screen. "Hey, Megan."

"It's Jack. Are you at Ben's?"

Luke frowned. "Yes, and why are you using your sister's phone?"

"I think Kate's in labor. Can you swing by here now?"

"I'm on my way." He disconnected the call. "Kate's in labor."

Ben stopped peeling and looked up. "How will you get to Sunny Ridge?"

"Are all the roads closed?"

"We're surrounded by a ring of fire. You'll have to drive south toward the Victorian border."

"Can we get through to Albury?"

His brother nodded. "If you do a long loop south to the Murray River at Jingellic. The roads are clear from Albury to Sunny Ridge."

Luke snatched his car keys off the kitchen counter. "That sounds like a good option, and we can head over the border to the hospital in Wodonga if her labor progresses too fast."

"You'll be okay once you're on the highway to Sunny Ridge and can call an ambulance to meet you. Is there anything I can do?"

He shook his head, walking with Ben to the back door. "Pray we make it to a hospital on time."

Ben slapped his back. "You've delivered a baby before."

"In a hospital. I don't want to deliver Kate's baby on the side of the road."

"That wouldn't be good, especially if there are complications. I'll be praying."

"Thanks. Say goodbye to Amy and the kids for me."

Luke drove to Jack's farm in record time, parked on the drive and grabbed his medical bag from the backseat.

Jack raced over to meet him, concern etched on his face. "Thanks for coming over."

"How's Kate doing?"

Jack shoved his hand through his hair. "She seems calm but I can tell she's in a fair bit of pain."

He walked with Jack to the house. "Do you know if her waters have broken?"

"Not yet, and her contractions have slowed a little bit."

"Okay." He climbed the steps to the back deck, his gaze homing in on Kate.

Kate paced along the polished wooden floor, her steps heavy. She gave Luke a tight smile. "I'm glad to see you."

"I'm glad I was nearby. How long have you had the contractions?"

"They started before breakfast."

Jack let out an exasperated breath. "Why didn't you say something earlier?"

"Because they were only twinges and weren't close together."

Luke nodded. "We need to go inside and I'll check you over. Is Megan around?"

"Yes." Kate rubbed her belly with both hands. "She's inside with Doris, and they're trying to contact Jack's parents."

"Okay. Let's see what's happening with this baby." He followed Jack and Kate indoors, relieved Kate's contractions had slowed. It looked as though they'd have time to reach Sunny Ridge before the baby decided it wanted to be born.

Megan sat on the sofa beside Doris and disconnected her phone call to her parents. "They won't be back for at least a few hours."

Doris sipped her tea. "You should go to the hospital with Kate and Jack while I wait here."

"Will you be okay on your own?"

"The fires aren't a threat to the farm, and we can drive over to Sunny Ridge later tonight. The baby may not even arrive until tomorrow."

"True."

Luke appeared in the doorway, worry lines prominent between his eyebrows.

Megan leaped to her feet. "Have you seen Kate? How's she doing?"

Luke smiled, his gaze softening. "She's doing great, and getting ready to leave for the hospital."

"Now?" Megan asked.

"It's going to take four or five hours to reach Sunny Ridge," he said.

"That's not good news." Doris fluffed up a cushion on the sofa. "Which route are you planning to take?"

"Along the Murray."

Megan twisted a lock of hair around her finger. "That's the long way around."

He nodded. "So far there are no fire outbreaks on that route. We could wait a few hours and hope the roads into town reopen, but there's another large fire to the west that's blocking the roads between Snowgum Creek and Sunny Ridge."

"Okay, that makes sense." Megan bit her lower lip. "Do you want me to come with you?"

"Yes, please. Another pair of hands will be helpful if we don't make it to the hospital in time."

She covered her mouth with her hand. "Is that likely?"

He shrugged. "Babies are unpredictable."

Doris stood. "I'll help you organize your supplies for the road."

"Thanks," Luke said. "We'll need towels and a bucket in case Kate throws up. Jack's filling a large flask of water and topping up my Jeep with fuel."

"I'm on it." Doris walked out of the room.

Luke held Megan's gaze and stepped closer. "We need to talk later."

"I know." She lowered her lashes. "Kate's baby is our first priority now."

Kate wandered into the room, her eyes glazed. "We're nearly ready to go."

Megan frowned. "You don't look too good."

"I'm okay." Kate sighed. "I took Luke's advice and I'm wearing my least favorite maternity dress."

Megan cringed. "We're hoping and praying we'll get you to the hospital in time and you won't deliver the baby in the car."

Luke clapped his hands together. "It's time to hit the road. The hospital is expecting us tonight."

Megan turned to Luke. "Are we traveling together, or do you want me to bring my car?"

"We'll go together because I may need your help."

"Yes, Megan," Kate said. "You can sit in the front with Luke while Jack looks after me in the back."

"Sure." Megan collected her purse from the coffee table. "Let's go."

She had at least four hours to survive in the car with Luke, knowing she hadn't made a decision about the job. He was determined to talk and she had no idea what to say. The thought of walking away from him was growing harder to accept. But how could she turn down a remarkable career opportunity and the chance to travel the world?

Minutes later Megan buckled her seat belt and slouched in the familiar front passenger seat in Luke's Jeep. Kate sat in the middle of the back seat, her head resting on Jack's shoulder.

Luke revved the engine. "Who wants to pray before we leave?"

"I will," Megan said.

Luke held her gaze and released the hand brake. "Thanks."

She closed her eyes. "Lord, please keep us safe as we take Kate to the hospital. We pray that the baby will be patient and wait until we reach Sunny Ridge Hospital. Please help Kate to cope with the pain and discomfort. And please give us a good run on the back roads to the highway, with no new fires flaring up to slow us down. Amen."

"Amen." Luke patted her hand and turned onto the road heading south. "We'll get there in time."

"I hope so." She glanced over her shoulder. Kate's eyes were shut, her face creased as if she was in the middle of enduring another painful contraction.

Luke bumped up the air-conditioning and cold air blasted through the cabin. "Is Kate okay?"

"Yes." Jack placed a damp cloth on his wife's forehead. "My girl is doing well."

Kate groaned. "I'll be glad when the long drive is over and this baby is out."

The first hour of the trip passed quickly. Luke and Jack amused Kate by telling her stories from their teenage years. Megan half listened, her mind dwelling on her job dilemma. She had less than forty-eight hours to make a decision, and no clue how to discern the right option. She'd spent an hour reading her Bible last night, and if anything she was more confused than before.

A mass of white appeared on the road ahead. "Luke, watch out for the sheep."

"I see them." He slowed the Jeep, crawling to a halt as a flock of sheep gathered across the road.

Megan huffed. "What are these silly sheep doing on the road?"

"They're grazing by the side of the road," Luke said.

Kate sighed. "Please tell me they'll move soon."

Luke rolled the Jeep forward. "Megan, can you please hop out and walk ahead to try and keep them moving?"

She rolled her eyes. "Sure, but you know it probably won't work too well."

He grinned. "I always wanted to see you round up sheep."

Jack laughed. "I'd help you but Kate needs me."

"Yeah, as if you'd help. You just want another funny story about me to add to your collection."

She didn't wait for a response, leaping out of the vehicle and onto the gravel road.

The sheep gave her an inquisitive look. A number of young lambs stayed close to their mothers.

"Okay, I need you all to move off the road." She stepped forward, avoiding the sheep droppings in her path. "The mama sheep among you should understand that I have a pregnant sister-in-law in the car who needs to deliver her baby soon."

She waved her hands in front of her, and the sheep circled back around her. A few peeled off the road, and Luke crawled along in the Jeep behind her.

"That's right, we're going to get out of the way and not become roadkill for the crows."

The sheep wandered in confused loops, mimicking her decision process regarding the research job.

She quickened her pace and worked her way to the front of the flock. The sheep ran all over the road, a few narrowly missing being hit by the Jeep.

She glanced back at Luke.

He pointed at her and laughed.

She tipped her nose in the air and continued forward, making progress. The sun beat down on her face, and a hint of smoke lingered in the air.

She moved to the side of the road and Luke brought the Jeep to a halt. She climbed back in, a sheen of perspiration on her face.

He grinned. "Good job."

"Yeah, whatever." She pulled her seat belt over her shoulder. "Kate, how are you doing?"

"The same. Thanks for clearing the sheep."

"No worries."

Jack chuckled. "You could get a new job as a shepherd."

Megan poked her tongue out at her brother. "Very funny."

Before long the Murray River came into view, and they followed the meandering waterway for half an hour before heading back into the pastureland surrounded by forest.

Luke braked as they approached an intersection. "We're not far from the Hume Highway. Kate, are you okay to keep going to Sunny Ridge, or do you want to detour south into Albury? The hospital across the river in Wodonga has a maternity ward."

Kate groaned. "I think I'm okay. I'd rather go to Sunny Ridge and try to follow my birth plan with my doctor."

Luke tapped his fingers on the steering wheel. "Are the contractions any closer together?"

"Not really. It's about the same. I think you're safe from having to do the delivery."

Megan let out a deep breath. "That's a relief." She hadn't been looking forward to the mess and chaos of a road-side birth.

Luke smiled. "I'm glad to hear it."

Megan stared out the window at the passing scenery, counting down the minutes until they reached Sunny Ridge and she found herself alone with Luke. He wasn't going to let her off the hook, and she couldn't avoid the inevitable conversation about her future.

Luke slowed his speed as they cruised into the outskirts of Sunny Ridge, the streetlights glowing in the night sky. After giving Kate a brief stop at a rest area off the highway, they had made good time to Sunny Ridge. Megan was quiet beside him, looking deep in thought.

Kate grunted and wriggled in her seat. "I'm glad we're nearly at the hospital."

He glanced over his shoulder. "Are the contractions stronger and faster?"

"Yep," Kate said.

"Don't forget your breathing. We'll be at the hospital in less than five minutes."

"Thanks, Luke." Jack wiped a loose strand of hair back off Kate's damp forehead. "We appreciate your help."

"You're welcome, and I'm glad we'll get there in time."

"Me, too," Megan said.

He snuck a sideways glimpse at Megan, small frown

lines forming between her brows. What was going on inside her head? Had she made a decision?

Luke drove into the main hospital entry. "Jack, are you able to take Kate inside while we park?"

"Sure," Jack said. "Why don't you two go to the café? I'll message you when we have some news."

Luke nodded and opened his car door. "That works for us."

Jack helped Kate step down onto the sidewalk, her discomfort evident on her weary face.

Luke met Jack's concerned gaze. "You've made it, and Kate will be in good hands now."

"Thanks again." Jack hitched Kate's bag over his shoulder and drew his wife close to his side as they headed into the hospital.

Luke parked his vehicle and they climbed out. He walked in silence with Megan to the café near the maternity ward.

He paused in the doorway. "Do you feel like dinner? I'm hungry."

She nodded. "Sounds good. My appetite has returned now I know Kate and the baby are here and safe."

He rolled his shoulders, the tension from the long drive cramping his back and neck muscles. "What do you feel like?"

"Chicken schnitzel."

He did a double take. "Really? That's my favorite from this café, too."

"Emily got me into it. We usually meet here for lunch each week."

"Ah, that makes sense. She really likes her schnitzel, drowned in gravy."

"Yep. I take it easy on the gravy."

They walked over to the counter and placed their orders for schnitzel before selecting a table near a window.

Megan played with a paper napkin, folding it in different configurations.

He stretched in his chair, feeling as if he was heading into his usual Saturday night shift with a deficit of sleep. How had this weekend become so exhausting?

"I like meeting Emily here," Megan said. "She has been really helpful to talk to about a lot of stuff."

"That's good." He rested his chin in his hands, his gaze homing in on her. "Have you made a decision?"

"Not yet. I still have time."

He shook his head. "The clock is ticking and Bruce needs an answer." And he needed an answer, too! Why couldn't she realize that her procrastination was messing with his head? He was over waiting for her to make up her mind. Either she was in or she was out. She loved him enough to stay or she sought her freedom.

"I do know this." She tucked her hair behind her ears. "I'm trying to work it all out."

He let out a frustrated breath. "It's really quite simple. You either want the big research career or you want to explore a more serious relationship with me. You can't have both."

"Can't you see that's why this decision is so hard? I don't want to leave you or Snowgum Creek."

The quiet desperation in her words deflated some of his aggravation. "I don't want you to stay and live with regrets. Or wake up in ten years feeling discontented and wondering where your life would be if you'd done the master's degree."

"I get it, but I'm still blown away by the opportunity to work with Bruce and his team."

"Will a satisfying career give you a happy and fulfilling life?"

"Maybe. Maybe not."

A waiter arrived with their food.

Luke's stomach grumbled and he tucked into his dinner, savoring the tasty chicken dish.

Megan bent her head and focused on eating. She didn't make eye contact with him and ignored her latte.

Luke swallowed a mouthful of schnitzel, unwilling to wait for her to initiate further conversation. "Why did you return to Snowgum Creek?"

She looked up, her startled eyes meeting his gaze. "Why does it matter?"

"There are a million other things you could have done. I really think the key to working out what you want to do with your life is to understand why you felt compelled to return to your hometown."

She nodded, switching her focus to the folded-up napkin beside her plate.

"And avoiding Jason doesn't count as a reason. You could have easily traveled overseas and guaranteed that you wouldn't run into him. If anything, Snowgum Creek was a risky option in that respect."

"True." She cleared her throat. "Jason knew where I grew up."

"Exactly. And let me ask another question. How does your faith factor into your decision-making process?"

"I've been praying about this decision and reading my Bible."

He nodded. "You've settled back into the close-knit church community in Snowgum Creek, and you have a number of good friends there as well as your family. Are you prepared to move away from them, and risk losing the close friendships you've developed?"

She shook her head. "We can all still be friends, even if I'm not living in Snowgum Creek."

"But it's not the same when you're not in regular contact. Life moves on, people change and evolve." He looked her straight in the eye. "I'm not going to put my life on hold and wait for you to return."

She gasped. "I would never expect you to do that."

"Then you need to know what you're losing if you walk away."

Her phone beeped and she checked the screen. "Jack said Kate is doing well and the baby will be born very soon." Her eyes brightened. "I'm going to become an aunt tonight."

Chapter 15

Megan typed a short reply to Jack's message in her phone, her hands shaky. She couldn't wait to meet the baby.

Luke continued to eat his chicken schnitzel. "Did Jack give you any details?"

"No, he'll contact us when the baby is born and they're ready for visitors." She placed her phone on the table. "I asked him not to tell me if bub is a boy or a girl."

"You want a surprise?"

She nodded. "We're only a few minutes away, and I can wait until I see them in person."

"Sure." He placed his cutlery on his empty plate. "You realize we still could have a few hours to wait."

"I hope not." She sipped her latte, avoiding Luke's forthright gaze. His words from earlier hammered away in her head. If she accepted the research job, she could say farewell to any possibility of a long-term relationship with Luke. She swallowed the milky coffee, her throat tight. Could she leave Luke a second time, knowing there was no turning back?

He held his coffee mug in both hands. "I've been thinking about going on a short-term mission trip overseas."

She looked up, shocked by his words. "When?"

"I don't know yet. I haven't thought that far ahead."

"Where do you want to go?"

"The aid organizations are always looking for doctors to volunteer in developing countries." He sipped his latte. "Unlike you, I haven't traveled a lot overseas."

"But you've been to a few places."

"New Zealand, Hawaii and Bali, but they were all short holidays squeezed in around my work schedule."

She tilted her head to the side. "I didn't know you wanted to travel."

"You never asked." He stretched out in his seat. "I've spent years studying and working all the time, and I've come to realize that there's more to life than work."

"I agree."

"I think it's time I started broadening my horizons."

"That makes sense." If only she could discern the best option for her future. Could she give up the research opportunity with no regrets?

Her phone beeped and she glanced at the screen. "It's my mother." She scanned the message. "The fires are under control and the roads from Snowgum Creek have reopened. My mom and Doris are half an hour away, and my father is not far behind them in Kate's car."

"I'm glad your family will be here tonight."

She nodded. "Would you like another coffee?"

"I'm good, but don't let me stop you."

She rested her arms on the table. "All this waiting around is starting to drive me crazy."

He chuckled. "You've never had much patience."

"I know." She glanced at the time on her phone. "When is this baby going to be born?"

"When he or she is ready."

"Ugh. I really don't like this waiting business."

"We've been here less than two hours, and it's kind of normal for me to be hanging around a hospital on a Saturday night."

She groaned. "I'm sorry you're stuck here tonight."

"It's okay. I'm not sorry I'm stuck here with you."

She blinked, warmth gliding up her neck and flushing her cheeks. His words gave her hope. At least his initial anger over her secret had lessened, and he was prepared to give her more time.

Her phone beeped again. Jack. She read his message and gasped.

Luke grinned. "Bub has arrived."

"Yes, I'm so excited. Jack has sent me all the baby statistics, excluding the gender." She curved her lips into a big smile. "Kate and the baby are doing well, and we can visit in around fifteen minutes."

"That's great news."

"I can't wait to see them." She stood. "I need to go and get myself photo ready."

He rolled his eyes. "You look fine."

"Only fine?"

"Fishing for compliments, are we?"

"Only from you."

His eyes twinkled. "That's the right answer."

She laughed. "I'll be back soon." She strode over to the bathroom, her step light. No doubt she needed to freshen up her makeup after a long day of traveling and waiting around the hospital.

Fifteen minutes later Megan strolled with Luke into the maternity ward reception area. The midwives recognized them, and they chatted for a couple of minutes before being led to a private room.

Megan opened the door and her gaze homed in on Kate holding a tiny bundle in her arms. "Wow."

Jack stood and stepped toward her, a wide smile lighting up her brother's face. "We have a daughter."

"Congratulations." She hugged her brother, happiness welling up inside her. "She's tiny."

Kate cooed at her baby, her gaze tender. "She's perfect, and a good size considering she's two weeks early."

Luke shook Jack's hand. "Congratulations. I'm glad to hear everything went well in the end."

"Thanks." Jack stifled a yawn. "It's been a long day but Kate was brilliant. I'm in awe of her and what she has accomplished today."

Kate looked up, catching her husband's loving gaze. "I couldn't have done it without you."

Jack reached for his wife's hand. "You look wonderful, considering what you've been through."

Megan stood on the other side of the bed beside Kate. "Does my little niece have a name?"

Kate nodded. "Sarah. We haven't decided on a middle name."

"I like it." Megan's gaze rested on Sarah, named after one of Kate's oldest and dearest friends who lived in England. "How's baby Sarah doing?"

"She was hungry earlier, and has dozed off after having a good feed," Kate said. "I'm not surprised she's sleepy."

Megan turned to Jack. "Mom and Dad should be here soon."

Jack smiled. "They just sent me a message and told me to be prepared for lots of photos."

"Yes, I have my phone ready." Megan's gaze lingered on her niece, wrapped up in muslin. "She looks so peaceful."

"I hope it's a sign she'll be an easy baby." Kate dropped a kiss on her daughter's head. "Would you like to hold her?"

"Yes, please," Megan said. "I can't remember the last time I cuddled a newborn."

Luke moved to her side. "Make sure you support her head."

"Okay." She furrowed her brow. "Since you're the doctor and used to handling babies, can you pass her over to me?"

"Sure." Luke gathered Sarah in his arms and gave her an indulgent smile. "She's adorable."

Megan's heart softened, the tender look on Luke's face stirring up unfamiliar feelings. He'd make a wonderful father one day. She could see him as the father of her children, holding her precious baby in his arms.

She bit her lip, disconcerted by the direction of her thoughts. Was this her destiny? The life that she really wanted, and the reason she was compelled earlier in the year to return to Snowgum Creek?

Megan lifted her arm and Luke placed Sarah in the crook of her elbow. She drew the baby close to her body and her heart melted, an intense love for the helpless infant flowing through her. "She's beautiful. I love her scrunched-up little face."

Luke chuckled. "She's looking pretty good. Some babies look a bit beaten-up when they're first born."

"I'm totally in love with my niece." Sarah's tiny hand escaped from the muslin, her delicate fingers wriggling as if she was waking up. Megan let out a deep sigh, her maternal instincts kicking into overdrive. One day she wanted to have a precious baby of her own to love and nurture.

Luke leaned back against the wall in Kate's hospital room, fascinated by the transformation taking place on Megan's gorgeous face as she held her niece. Megan's soft, loving gaze was protective, and she dropped a kiss on Sarah's forehead.

Jack laughed. "I never thought I'd see the day."

Megan lifted a brow. "Huh?"

"My sister is clucky."

Kate giggled. "That's so true. Jack, take a photo of Megan with Sarah."

Luke shuffled to the other side of the room, out of camera range.

Jack snapped a couple of photos of the proud aunt with her niece. Luke's heart skipped a beat, imagining Megan holding her own baby. His child.

He rubbed his hand over his face, the fleeting image bittersweet. By Monday he'd know if that was ever going to be possible. She held his future in her hands, and didn't seem to realize or care about how her indecisive actions were wreaking havoc in his life.

Kate waved at him. "Luke, please stand with Megan so we can get a photo of the four of you."

Luke moved to Megan's side, his arm only inches away from her. Sarah gurgled and her tiny face puckered.

Kate snapped a few photos and he walked away from Megan, thankful to have some distance. His delight for his friends was tempered by his frustration with Megan. He detested living in limbo, his life on hold until she made up her mind.

A knock sounded on the door, and Megan's parents entered the room with Doris. Megan passed Sarah to her mother, and the family gathered around the newborn.

Luke caught Jack's eye. "I think I'll take off now, if that's okay with you?"

"Sure." Jack smiled. "We really appreciate everything you've done for us today."

Megan moved to Luke's side. "Are you leaving now?"

He nodded. "Your family's here, and you can catch a lift back with them to Snowgum Creek later. I don't want to intrude on your family time."

She pressed her lips together. "I'll be in touch tomorrow, but I don't know if I'll make it to morning church if we stay here late."

He nodded. "Can we talk tomorrow?"

"Yes." She gulped in a shallow breath. "I promise I will make my decision by tomorrow."

"Okay." He said his goodbyes to Megan's family and walked out of the room. The familiar corridor crowded in on him, the intensity of the past few hours catching up with him. He swung by the café and purchased a coffee to go. He looked forward to having two hours by himself on the drive home to think and pray.

Lord, is my desire to marry Megan and build a family with her an impossible dream?

For his sanity he needed to end the madness tomorrow, and make a decision one way or the other. He loved Megan but he couldn't live with her constant indecisiveness. She needed to either commit to a relationship with him or walk away. The middle ground was no longer an option.

A few hours later, Megan headed back down the corridor to the hospital café. She'd arranged to meet Emily during her break. She had left her parents and Doris coddling Kate and Sarah, doting on their first grandchild.

Jack had fallen asleep in the reclining chair beside Kate's bed. Sarah was a content baby, and the midwives were happy with her progress. Her family planned to drive home to Snowgum Creek after she caught up with Emily.

Emily breezed into the café, her blond hair tied up in a knot at the back of her head. "Hey, Megan." She hugged her close, a big smile on her face. "Congratulations on becoming an aunt."

Megan grinned. "I'm pretty excited. Sarah is so cute."

"I'm sure she is. I'll swing by Kate's room with you

before I go back on night duty." Emily glanced at her phone. "I have twenty-five minutes left of my break, and I'm starving."

Megan walked to the counter with Emily and ordered a latte to go. Emily requested a club sandwich with her coffee and they sat at their usual table in the corner.

Emily devoured half her sandwich, and wiped a dab of mayo off the corner of her mouth with a napkin. "Where's Luke?"

"He left when my parents and Doris arrived."

Emily's eyes widened. "You haven't made a decision about the job."

"Not yet."

"Megan, you can't keep doing this to Luke. It's not fair and you know it."

She bit her lip, tears pricking her eyes. "I can't bear the thought of leaving him."

"Then don't leave him." Emily sighed, her tone soothing. "Tell him how you feel and that you want to stay with him in Snowgum Creek."

"You're right."

"Of course I'm right." Emily took another bite of her sandwich, her gaze thoughtful. "I know Luke, and his love for you is genuine. The real deal. There aren't too many men like him out there. And the worst thing is you'll break his heart if you leave him again."

She sipped her latte. "I know and I've been praying about this."

"I think you have your answer. You can trust Luke to love you forever and do his best to be a good husband. His faith is strong and he has his priorities right."

"I know." Luke's faith was rock solid, unlike hers, which had wavered in the breeze since she'd left university. The past few months in Snowgum Creek had shown her the importance of making her faith and family her priority.

"Good." Emily gulped down a mouthful of coffee. "He has been waiting to find the right woman, one who shares his faith and values."

Emily's words resonated in her mind. Luke had made it clear that he wasn't going to settle for second best. And he was a natural at baby cuddling, stirring her maternal instincts. "I'll never forget holding Sarah for the first time."

"Yeah?"

Megan relaxed in her seat, her mouth lifting into a smile. "It was a beautiful moment, cradling this tiny baby who inspired so much love from everyone in the room."

"Babies often have that effect on people."

She nodded. "Emily, I think I've known for a long time what I should do. I knew, deep down, that I loved Luke and wanted to marry him. But I've always had a hard time sticking with things, making hard decisions and taking responsibility. I was afraid I would miss out on something if I settled down in one place.

"But being back in church, being with my family and Luke, and now having baby Sarah, it's all put it in perspective for me. I can see how empty my life was before. I'm still a little afraid, but I don't want to let Luke go. Like you said, there aren't too many men like him. In fact, I haven't met any."

Emily grinned. "I'm so glad you've worked this out."

"You knew I was going to choose Luke?"

"You two are a good match, and I believe God brought you back together for a reason. And just remember, being married doesn't mean you stop living and doing fun things. You can still travel and ski. But now you'll always have a place to come home to."

Megan pressed her finger on the corner of her eye, a tear

trying to escape from beneath her lashes. "Now I need to convince him that he still wants to marry me, despite the fact I've been a complete idiot."

Emily laughed. "I don't think that's going to be too hard. The man is head over heels in love with you."

Megan's heart filled with hope, overflowing with love for Luke and her niece.

Lord, thank You for providing wise friends like Emily and Kate. And for the safe arrival of Sarah. Please help me to have the right words to express my feelings to Luke tomorrow. I pray he'll forgive me for not realizing this earlier.

Chapter 16

Megan adjusted the rim of her sunglasses on her nose, quickening her pace as she walked along the main street in Snowgum Creek. She'd slept through her alarm this morning, struggling to wake from her restless night's sleep. After arriving back late last night from the hospital, she'd been unable to switch off her overactive mind. Church had started five minutes ago and she'd messaged Luke, asking him to save her a seat near the back.

The skirt of her long cotton dress swirled around her legs in the light breeze, her feet clad in comfortable sandals for her brisk walk. She crossed the road and entered the church, thankful the congregation were on their feet and singing. The whole church wouldn't notice her tardiness.

Luke caught her eye, and she squeezed into the vacant seat beside him.

He smiled. "Good to see you."

"You, too." She switched her attention to the overhead screen, singing along with the congregation.

Luke stood tall, looking relaxed and refreshed. An uninterrupted night's sleep because he wasn't on call at the hospital last night seemed to have made a big difference. She'd gulped down half a cup of coffee and a slice of toast this morning before rushing out the door.

The song ended and she sat down, comforted by Luke's

arm resting beside hers. It felt right to be by his side in church, surrounded by their friends. Amy's father stood at the podium, working his way through the announcements and notices. Her ears pricked up when her pastor mentioned her family's name.

"We're delighted to hear that Jack and Kate Bradley are celebrating the birth of baby Sarah, born last night in Sunny Ridge. I also heard it was a bit of an adventure to get Kate to the hospital due to all the fires. We're thankful the fires are now under control, and Kate and Sarah are doing well. Please remember the Bradley family in your prayers."

Megan smiled as she reflected on her pastor's words. The congregation cared about her family, and a strong sense of belonging seeped into her heart.

Luke squeezed her hand and whispered in her ear, "I'm sure half the congregation has already seen the baby photos."

She nodded. "My mother started sharing a few photos last night."

The service passed slowly, and she struggled to keep her eyes open during the sermon. Her pastor talked about priorities in the Christian life, and how God needed to be number one in our lives.

Her eyelids fluttered closed, her mind dwelling on her career decision. If she had accepted the research job, would her desire to prioritize her career have created problems in her relationship with God? Or could she have remained strong in her faith if she returned to her carefree and nomadic lifestyle?

Her past history suggested she'd stumble without the steady support of her close friends and church family. She had drifted along, distracted by the pursuit of worldly goals and dreams.

She opened her eyes, Jesus's words from the Gospel of Mark stirring her heart. How could she love the Lord above everyone and everything else, including Luke and her career? What would her life look like if she chose this path?

Before long the service ended and Luke turned to her.

"You look exhausted," he said.

She winced. "I've had a lot on my mind."

"Do you want to stay here a bit longer, or take a walk in the park?"

"A walk sounds good, after we pick up a coffee to go."

He grinned. "You haven't had your caffeine fix this morning?"

"Is it that obvious?"

"Yes, but understandable. Are you heading back to the hospital today?"

She shook her head. "Mom and Dad will probably visit this afternoon, and Kate should be home with Sarah in the next few days."

Megan snuck out the main door of the church with Luke, accepting baby congratulations from their pastor and well-wishers. Her parents and Doris hadn't made it to church this morning. No doubt they were exhausted after their busy day and long trip to the hospital late yesterday afternoon.

She walked in silence with Luke across the road to the bakery, the sun warming her face. She stifled a yawn, looking forward to an injection of caffeine to wake her up. They ordered lattes and doughnuts, waiting only a few minutes for their coffee before heading back across the road to the park.

Luke pointed to a bench in the shade under a canopy of gum trees. "Would you like to sit here?"

"Sure." The bench was a number of steps off the main path, giving them privacy to talk without being overheard by passersby.

He sat beside her, offering a doughnut from the paper bag. "I still can't believe you wanted a doughnut."

"They look good." She selected a chocolate one and placed it on a napkin.

He shook his head. "We haven't eaten doughnuts together in years."

She shrugged and sipped her coffee. "I need a sugar hit to keep me going."

"Did you sleep at all last night?"

"Kind of. I think I tossed and turned most of the night." She bit into the cream-filled donut, savoring the sweet texture and chocolate flavor. "I've made my decision."

He paused, holding his doughnut in midair. "You've told Bruce."

"Not yet." She tipped her chin up, meeting his questioning gaze. "I'm not taking the research job."

Luke's stomach flipped as Megan's announcement sank in. "You're saying no to the opportunity."

"Yep." She smiled, her eyes soft. "And I feel at peace about my decision."

He took a sip of his drink and turned toward her, shifting a few inches closer on the park bench. A glimmer of hope stirred in his heart. Could they build a future together? Was she prepared to commit to living in a small town?

He leaned against the hard bench seat, bracing his forearm on top of the wooden slats. "What led you to this decision?"

She flicked her hair back over her shoulders. "I finally figured out my priorities."

"Which are?"

"My faith is a lot stronger now. I no longer feel like I'm in the wilderness, wandering aimlessly and searching for more meaning in my life."

"Okay." This sounded promising, but he reined in his hopeful thoughts. He needed to be sure that she was making this decision for the right reasons.

She bit into her doughnut, and licked cream off her upper lip. "A few months ago I wouldn't have indulged in one of these."

"Because of your healthy eating regimen."

"Yes, I admit I was obsessive about my diet and exercise program. It was the most important aspect of my life, and I couldn't bear to miss an exercise session."

"So what's changed?" He shot her a cheeky grin. "Are you going to start eating a doughnut every day?"

She laughed. "Not quite, but the world isn't going to end if I break my diet rules or miss a couple of exercise sessions."

"The rest of us already knew that."

"Very funny. Do you know why I didn't go to the ski fields last season?"

He tipped his head to the side. "No, but I had wondered why you didn't seem interested, especially after the situation with Jason was resolved."

She pressed her lips together. "I was scared that if I went back I wouldn't want to leave."

"I had no idea you missed skiing that much." The research job was an attractive proposition, combining her love of skiing with an academic career.

"I don't want to go back to my old life, or get caught up in an all-consuming career that will leave little time for anything else."

Luke nodded. "I totally get the work thing. As you know, I'm seeking balance in my life as well, and also trying to avoid filling all the gaps for everyone else at the expense of my own health and well-being."

She looked up, staring into his eyes. "You should feel

like you can give yourself permission to travel and do mission work overseas, if the opportunity is there."

"True. What opportunities do you think are opening up for you?"

"Careerwise I can stay in Snowgum Creek. I find my jobs here fulfilling, and I don't need to chase academic accolades to feel like I'm a success."

He widened his eyes. "Don't you think your career so far is successful?"

"Not really. I've floated around between jobs but haven't truly committed to anything, until this year."

He reached for her hand, trailing his thumb along her fingertips. "Are you serious about having commitment in other areas of your life?"

She nodded. "I want to spend more time with my family. I want to have the opportunity to get to know Sarah and be a part of her life. To do that I need to live closer to Snowgum Creek. Sydney is too far away. And I'd like to see more of Jack and Kate now they're new parents."

"I'm sure they'll appreciate your support."

She sucked in a deep breath. "I know I did the wrong thing by not telling you about Bruce's offer. And I need to have the courage to speak up and discuss the tough issues."

"You know you can trust me."

She squeezed his hand. "You're too good for me."

He shook his head. "I'm far from perfect and we all make mistakes."

"Can you forgive me?"

"Yes." He cupped her cheek in his hand, gazing into her beautiful eyes. "I hope you're willing to give us another chance, because I love you, Megan Bradley."

She leaned closer, her magnetic eyes locked with his. "I love you, Luke Morton, and I don't plan on leaving Snowgum Creek anytime soon."

He lowered his head, his lips caressing her sweet mouth. She ran her fingers through his hair and he drew her closer, deepening the kiss. Moments later he reluctantly pulled back, breaking their connection.

He grinned. "I could sit here and kiss you all afternoon."

She laughed. "I don't have to be anywhere this afternoon."

He draped his arm over her shoulders, inhaling the light floral scent in her hair. The birds in the overhead branches sang, and he sighed. A perfect way to spend a Sunday afternoon, with the woman he loved in his arms.

Megan removed her sandals at Luke's front door and walked ahead of him into his new house. Luke was only a few weeks away from moving in, and he'd been working on the finishing touches. The pool installation company was booked to start digging up the ground at the back of the house next week.

She smiled. "I love the color and tones. Your interior decorator has given you great advice."

Luke nodded. "I'm happy with the result. Modern but not over-the-top with too much color."

"But not too bland or beige, either." Her toes curled into the soft carpet underfoot as she toured the formal living areas.

He glanced at his watch. "I have something special to show you on the veranda."

"Sounds fun."

They returned to the front door and she slipped her heels back on her feet. Luke had mentioned dinner plans, and she wondered which restaurant he had in mind. Her sapphire bracelet glittered in the late-afternoon sunlight, a reminder of his generosity and the depth of his feelings for her.

Megan held Luke's hand and they strolled along the wide deck that wrapped around the house. Sweeping views over the town and mountains stole her breath. She could sit out here all day, admiring the incredible view.

"Unfortunately we will miss the sunset from this side, but it will be cool in summer and pick up the mountain breezes."

"True." The polished wooden decking gleamed underfoot. She rounded the corner and gasped. A white-linen-covered table for two was set up overlooking the mountains. Candles stood in the center of a pretty floral arrangement of miniature champagne roses.

"Oh, Luke, you didn't tell me we were having dinner here."

He gave her an indulgent smile. "Our dinner should arrive any minute."

"Really? What did you order?"

"Your favorites. I did my homework, and asked Kate and Jack for advice so I wouldn't get it wrong."

"They know about your plans?"

"And were sworn to secrecy." He pulled out a chair, helped her into her seat and sat in the chair beside her. He rolled up the sleeves of his shirt and poured two glasses of iced water.

She smoothed the long skirt of her navy blue dress over her legs, her curiosity piqued. A delivery van cruised up the drive, the Snowgum Creek Italian Restaurant logo on the door. Two waiters alighted from the vehicle, and assembled a trolley similar to the ones used for room service in hotels. A number of covered dinner plates were placed on the top and bottom levels of the four-wheel trolley.

"Wow, are we having silver service?"

"Only the best for my girl, and they'll be back in an hour with dessert."

She widened her eyes. "Tiramisu and gelato?"

"Of course. I told you I did my research."

Luke greeted the waiters, who brought the trolley to a halt beside their table.

A waiter placed a linen napkin on her lap, and slid a covered dinner plate on the table in front of her.

Luke smiled. "I took the liberty of skipping the starters, since their servings are generous. I ordered garlic bread and a side salad with balsamic vinaigrette."

"Sounds wonderful."

The waiters left and Luke reached for her hand. "Lord, thank You for this food, great company and my new house. Amen."

"Amen." She uncovered her plate, inhaling the delicious aroma of tomato and fresh herbs. "Vegetarian lasagna. I love this dish."

He lifted the stainless-steel lid off his plate, revealing a large serving of beef lasagna. "They do the best lasagna in town."

She savored the al dente pasta, enjoying the mushrooms, spinach and carrots in a rich tomato sauce.

"What's the verdict?" he asked.

"Delicious, as usual. I didn't know they home-delivered silver service."

"They don't." His eyes twinkled. "I called in a few favors, being a regular customer and prepared to pay for the additional services."

"I'm impressed." She picked at the green salad. "The ingredients are fresh and taste really good."

They chatted during their meal, enjoying the twilight falling over the mountains. She nibbled on the crunchy garlic bread, a perfect complement to the lasagna.

He placed his cutlery on his empty plate. "I wanted you to be the first person to share a meal here with me."

Her heart warmed. "This is really special, and you've gone to so much trouble."

He chuckled. "I have to compensate for the fact I can't cook."

Megan ate her last mouthful of lasagna. "There had to be something I can do better than you."

"You do lot of things better than me, like cycling."

She shrugged. "If you worked a little bit harder on your fitness, you'd easily pip me."

"Maybe." He placed a small velvet box on the table.

Her heart raced and she met his soft gaze. "Oh, Luke."

"Megan, I love you and I'm so blessed to have you back in my life." He dropped down on one knee, his gaze earnest as he held both of her hands. "Will you marry me?"

"Yes." She threw her arms around his neck, tears forming in the corners of her eyes. "I love you. I've always loved you, since we were at school together."

He cupped her face in his hands, staring deep into her eyes. "I love your enthusiastic yes, a big improvement on last time."

"My younger self wasn't smart enough to know what I was turning down."

"Would you like to see the ring?"

"Yes, I forgot about the ring."

He dragged his chair closer to her, and flipped open the velvet case. A square-cut diamond shimmered in the candlelight.

"Wow, this ring is so beautiful. I love the diamond."

He slid the ring on her finger, a perfect fit. "The princess cut seemed like an appropriate choice."

She dropped a kiss on his full lips. "I'm not a princess."

"You'll always be my princess and more. The woman I want to spend the rest of my life with, starting in our new house."

She looked around the veranda, the dusk shadows mingling with candlelight giving it a pretty glow. "I love your house."

"It's our home. I don't plan on moving in until after we get married."

She lifted a brow. "You want to wait? Or are we having a short engagement?"

"Jack made a few calls, and there are a number of reception venues with openings over summer. And the church isn't fully booked for the next few months, either."

"I need at least six weeks to organize a wedding."

"I'll give you eight, if that helps." He grinned. "But no longer."

"Okay, we'll have to wait and see if we can line everything up in time."

Luke nodded. "I need to ask Emily if she can work at the clinic so we can have a honeymoon. Or find someone else to cover for me."

"Do you really think we can pull this off in less than eight weeks?"

"I'd like to try." He slipped his arm around her shoulders and drew her closer, his lips exploring hers. "I've waited a long time for you to become my bride."

Breathless, she melted into his arms, her heart beating a fast staccato. Finally she was where she belonged with the man she loved.

Chapter 17

Megan stood outside the Snowgum Creek Community Church, the beading on her ivory silk strapless bridal gown shimmering in the late-afternoon sunshine. Her mother fussed over the train of her gown, baby Sarah tucked in her left arm.

Megan smiled. "Mom, let me hold Sarah."

Her mom wrinkled her nose. "She'll puke on your dress."

"I don't care." She reached for her niece. "I'd like one last cuddle before I walk down the aisle."

Her three-month-old niece, decked out in a pretty lilac floral dress with a matching bonnet, gave her a goofy smile. The photographer snapped a photo before returning her attention to the bridesmaids.

Kate laughed, holding her matron of honor bouquet of colorful pink and red roses plus Megan's champagne rose bouquet. "Look who loves her aunty Megan."

Megan's heart swelled, a desire for her own baby, a miniature version of Luke, building in her mind. "She's a good girl, and she wouldn't do anything to ruin my dress."

Megan's father glanced at his watch. "You'll be late if you don't join the girls now for the photos."

Megan handed Sarah back to her mother. She joined Kate, Rachel and Emily on the church steps, and followed the photographer's instructions. Her bridesmaids wore long burgundy silk dresses with tiny spaghetti straps, their hair loose around their shoulders.

Her mother strolled into the church with Sarah. A few minutes later Emily walked into the church, followed by Rachel.

Megan hugged Kate. "Thanks for all your help with the wedding."

Kate's smile widened. "You're welcome." She rearranged locks of Megan's hair around her bare shoulders, and pulled the veil forward over Megan's face. "I'm so excited that you and Luke are finally getting hitched."

Megan nodded, her grip tight on her fragrant bridal bouquet. "It's your turn to go inside."

Kate grinned. "I'll see you soon."

Megan stood with her father on the threshold, waiting for their cue to enter the church.

Her father tucked her arm through his. "I never thought I'd see the day that you'd settle down and get married."

"Well, it's here, and I can't wait to see Luke."

The tempo of the classical music piece slowed and Megan stepped into the church, clutching her father's arm. Her gaze homed in on Luke, standing tall beside Jack. Luke's brothers, Ben and Caleb, made up the numbers in the bridal party.

Luke gave her a dazzling smile, and a shiver of anticipation raced through her. He looked dashing in his three-piece suit, and she resisted the urge to run down the aisle to his side.

She smiled at their wedding guests, crowded into the rows of seats. Cameras flashed in all directions. She glided to the front of the church, reaching the last row and stepping forward with her father to stand beside Luke.

Luke held her hand and whispered in her ear. "You look breathtakingly beautiful, my gorgeous girl."

She twined her fingers with his, her breathing shallow. There was no turning back now.

Their pastor started talking and Megan's mind raced, the wedding ceremony seeming like a dream.

Before long she stood facing Luke, holding his hand as they repeated their vows. The sacred promises, made in God's sight, that represented her lifelong commitment to her husband. Megan spoke with confidence, her future with this incredible man bringing a huge smile to her lips.

The pastor pronounced them husband and wife. Luke lifted her veil back off her face, his golden eyes gleaming. "The moment I've been waiting for all day."

He curled his arm around her waist and drew her close, his warm lips possessive as he explored her mouth. Eyes closed, she surrendered to the kiss, her body relaxing against his as she reveled in their love.

The congregation broke out into loud applause, bringing her back to reality.

Luke pulled away, his gaze intense. "We'll have lots of time to finish this later."

She nodded, her face feeling flushed. "I can't wait."

Their pastor gave a short talk on love and commitment. Megan held Luke's loving gaze, thankful that God had brought them back together. She couldn't wait to start her new life as Luke's wife. The house was ready and they were moving in after a short honeymoon.

Before long they signed their wedding certificate with Jack and Kate as their witnesses, and they posed for more photos. The congregation sang the final song, Luke and Megan's favorite hymn from years ago, and it was time to walk out of the church.

Luke held her close to his side, his loving gaze heightening the warmth already coloring her cheeks. "I'm counting the hours until I have you all to myself."

Megan giggled. "Don't forget we need to enjoy our reception first."

"It will fly by, and then we'll have twelve uninterrupted days together."

"Are you finally going to tell me where we're going?"

His eyes sparkled. "Maui. We fly out of Sydney tomorrow night."

"Wow, I'm so excited!"

Megan walked back down the aisle with Luke, her steps light and her heart overflowing with love. She couldn't wait to honeymoon on the beach in Maui and take a break from their hectic schedules. The doctor had returned to her, and she treasured the opportunity to share her life with Luke in Snowgum Creek.

* * * * *

REQUEST YOUR FREE BOOKS!

2 FREE INSPIRATIONAL NOVELS
PLUS 2
FREE
MYSTERY GIFTS

Love Inspired®

YES! Please send me 2 FREE Love Inspired® novels and my 2 FREE mystery gifts (gifts are worth about $10). After receiving them, if I don't wish to receive any more books, I can return the shipping statement marked "cancel." If I don't cancel, I will receive 6 brand-new novels every month and be billed just $4.49 per book in the U.S. or $4.99 per book in Canada. That's a savings of at least 22% off the cover price. It's quite a bargain! Shipping and handling is just 50¢ per book in the U.S. and 75¢ per book in Canada.* I understand that accepting the 2 free books and gifts places me under no obligation to buy anything. I can always return a shipment and cancel at any time. Even if I never buy another book, the two free books and gifts are mine to keep forever.

105/305 IDN FVYV

Name _____ (PLEASE PRINT) _____

Address _____ Apt. # _____

City _____ State/Prov. _____ Zip/Postal Code _____

Signature (if under 18, a parent or guardian must sign)

Mail to the Harlequin® Reader Service:
IN U.S.A.: P.O. Box 1867, Buffalo, NY 14240-1867
IN CANADA: P.O. Box 609, Fort Erie, Ontario L2A 5X3

**Are you a subscriber to Love Inspired books
and want to receive the larger-print edition?
Call 1-800-873-8635 or visit www.ReaderService.com.**

* Terms and prices subject to change without notice. Prices do not include applicable taxes. Sales tax applicable in N.Y. Canadian residents will be charged applicable taxes. Offer not valid in Quebec. This offer is limited to one order per household. Not valid for current subscribers to Love Inspired books. All orders subject to credit approval. Credit or debit balances in a customer's account(s) may be offset by any other outstanding balance owed by or to the customer. Please allow 4 to 6 weeks for delivery. Offer available while quantities last.

Your Privacy—The Harlequin® Reader Service is committed to protecting your privacy. Our Privacy Policy is available online at www.ReaderService.com or upon request from the Harlequin Reader Service.
We make a portion of our mailing list available to reputable third parties that offer products we believe may interest you. If you prefer that we not exchange your name with third parties, or if you wish to clarify or modify your communication preferences, please visit us at www.ReaderService.com/consumerchoice or write to us at Harlequin Reader Service Preference Service, P.O. Box 9062, Buffalo, NY 14269. Include your complete name and address.

LIDIRI3

REQUEST YOUR FREE BOOKS!

2 FREE INSPIRATIONAL NOVELS
PLUS 2
FREE
MYSTERY GIFTS

Love Inspired

HISTORICAL
INSPIRATIONAL HISTORICAL ROMANCE

YES! Please send me 2 FREE Love Inspired® Historical novels and my 2 FREE mystery gifts (gifts are worth about $10). After receiving them, if I don't wish to receive any more books, I can return the shipping statement marked "cancel." If I don't cancel, I will receive 4 brand-new novels every month and be billed just $4.74 per book in the U.S. or $5.24 per book in Canada. That's a savings of at least 21% off the cover price. It's quite a bargain! Shipping and handling is just 50¢ per book in the U.S. and 75¢ per book in Canada.* I understand that accepting the 2 free books and gifts places me under no obligation to buy anything. I can always return a shipment and cancel at any time. Even if I never buy another book, the two free books and gifts are mine to keep forever.

102/302 IDN F5CY

Name	(PLEASE PRINT)	
Address		Apt. #
City	State/Prov.	Zip/Postal Code

Signature (if under 18, a parent or guardian must sign)

Mail to the Harlequin® Reader Service:
IN U.S.A.: P.O. Box 1867, Buffalo, NY 14240-1867
IN CANADA: P.O. Box 609, Fort Erie, Ontario L2A 5X3

Want to try two free books from another series?
Call 1-800-873-8635 or visit www.ReaderService.com.

* Terms and prices subject to change without notice. Prices do not include applicable taxes. Sales tax applicable in N.Y. Canadian residents will be charged applicable taxes. Offer not valid in Quebec. This offer is limited to one order per household. Not valid for current subscribers to Love Inspired Historical books. All orders subject to credit approval. Credit or debit balances in a customer's account(s) may be offset by any other outstanding balance owed by or to the customer. Please allow 4 to 6 weeks for delivery. Offer available while quantities last.

Your Privacy—The Harlequin® Reader Service is committed to protecting your privacy. Our Privacy Policy is available online at www.ReaderService.com or upon request from the Harlequin Reader Service.

We make a portion of our mailing list available to reputable third parties that offer products we believe may interest you. If you prefer that we not exchange your name with third parties, or if you wish to clarify or modify your communication preferences, please visit us at www.ReaderService.com/consumerchoice or write to us at Harlequin Reader Service Preference Service, P.O. Box 9062, Buffalo, NY 14269. Include your complete name and address.

LIHDIR13R

Rookie biographies®

Rachel Carson

By Justine and Ron Fontes

Consultant
Linda Bullock
Curriculum Specialist

Children's Press®
A Division of Scholastic Inc.
New York Toronto London Auckland Sydney
Mexico City New Delhi Hong Kong
Danbury, Connecticut

Designer: Herman Adler Design
Photo Researcher: Caroline Anderson
The photo on the cover shows Rachel Carson.

Library of Congress Cataloging-in-Publication Data

Fontes, Justine.
  Rachel Carson / by Justine & Ron Fontes.
    p. cm. — (Rookie biographies)
  Includes index.
  ISBN 0-516-25896-6 (lib. bdg.)   0-516-26819-8 (pbk.)
  1. Carson, Rachel, 1907-1964—Juvenile literature. 2. Biologists—United
States—Biography—Juvenile literature. 3. Environmentalists—United States—
Biography—Juvenile literature. I. Fontes, Ron. II. Title. III. Rookie biography.
  QH31.C33F66 2005
  570'.92—dc22

                                        2004015314

Do you love plants, animals, and the ocean?

This girl is holding a starfish.

This is Rachel Carson.

Rachel Carson did!

She wrote about plants and animals and how to take care of them.

Carson was born on May 27, 1907. She grew up on a farm in Pennsylvania.

Carson spent a lot of time with her little dog and her Mom.

This is Carson with her dog, Candy.

Carson looked at baby birds like these.

Carson's mother loved nature.
She taught Carson to look
closely at plants and animals.

So, Carson explored the woods
and creeks near her home.
Then she would ask questions
about what she saw.

Carson also learned from books and magazines. Her favorite magazine had stories that children wrote.

When Carson was ten, she wrote a story about a brave pilot. The magazine printed her story and gave Carson a prize!

ST NICHOLAS

FOR · BOYS · AND · GIRLS

SEPTEMBER · 1918

Carson's story was printed in this magazine.

Carson is dressed in her graduation cap and gown.

Carson kept writing stories and winning prizes. Everyone was sure she would become a writer.

In college, Carson decided to study nature instead. She studied hard and got good grades.

Many scientists work at Woods Hole Marine Biological Laboratory.

Carson studied nature at the Woods Hole Marine Biological Laboratory in Massachusetts.

There, she saw the ocean for the first time.

Carson used a typewriter to write stories.

16

Carson got a job writing radio shows about fish. She also wrote for magazines and newspapers.

Carson wrote every night after work. She wrote so well that she was asked to write a book.

Carson's first book was called *Under the Sea Wind*. She wrote about the many plants and animals that live in the ocean.

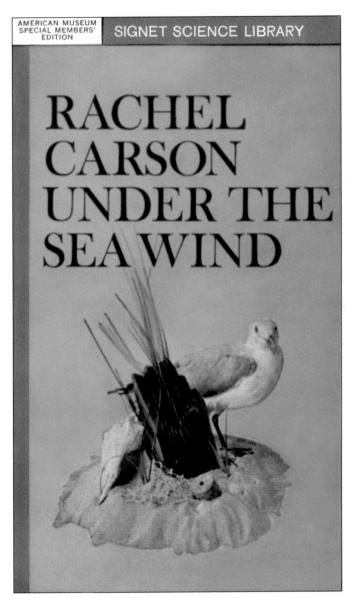

SIGNET SCIENCE LIBRARY

RACHEL CARSON UNDER THE SEA WIND

This is the cover of Carson's first book.

Scientists wore diving suits, like these, to explore the ocean.

Carson went underwater in a diving suit. She wanted to know what it was like to be a fish!

Carson also sailed on a research ship. She was the only woman scientist on the ship.

Carson wrote a second book. It was called *The Sea Around Us.*

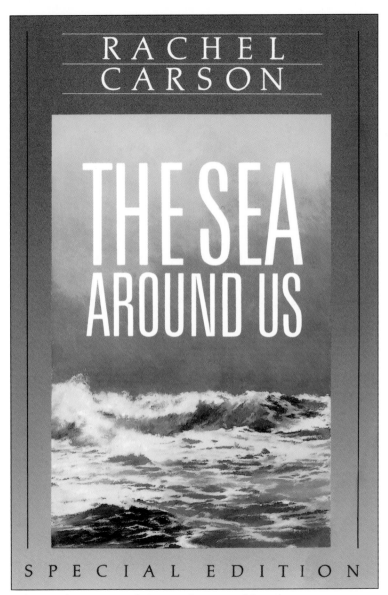

RACHEL
CARSON

THE SEA
AROUND US

SPECIAL EDITION

This is the cover of Carson's second book.

23

One day, Carson got a letter from her friend Olga. Olga had found dead birds in her yard. These birds were killed by bug poison.

Carson decided to study the poisons used to kill the bugs.

This farmer is spraying bug poison.

Carson found out that the poisons used to kill bugs killed other things, too.

She wrote a book called *Silent Spring*. The book was a warning about using poison.

Carson used a microscope to learn about many things.

John F. Kennedy was the 35th president of the United States.

Even the President listened
to Carson!

Soon there were laws to help keep the Earth and living things healthy. Carson helped make the world a better place.

Laws help protect birds and trees like these.

Words You Know

diving suits

magazine cover

poison

30

President John F. Kennedy

Rachel Carson

Index

About the Author

Justine and Ron Fontes have written over 350 children's books. They have written all kinds of books, both fiction and nonfiction. They are avid readers and supporters of nature. They live in Maine with three adorable cats.

Photo Credits

Photographs © 2005: AP/Wide World Photos: 28, 31 top; Beinecke Rare Book and Manuscript Library, Yale Collection of American Literature: 7, 12, 16; Corbis Images: 25, 30 bottom (William Gottlieb), 29 (Lynda Richardson); Dembinsky Photo Assoc./Sharon Cummings: 8; Magnum Photos/Erich Hartmann: cover, 4, 31 bottom; Used by permission of Oxford University Press, Inc.: 23 (book jacket from *The Sea Around Us*, by Rachel Carson, copyright 1950, 1951, 1961 by Rachel Carson, renewed by Roger Christie); Penguin Group USA: 19 (cover of *Under the Sea Wind*, by Rachel Carson, c 1941 Signet Science Library); PhotoEdit/Myrleen Ferguson Cate: 3; Rachel Carson Council, Inc./Brooks Studio: 27; St. Nicholas Magazine, For Boys and Girls, September, 1918, c 1918 by the Century Co.: 11, 30 top right; Superstock, Inc./ Underwood Photo Archives: 20, 30 top left; Time Life Pictures/Getty Images/ Fritz Goro: 14.